I0593994

Implicating Claudia

Books by Elle E. Kay

Faith Writes Publishing

ENDLESS MOUNTAIN SERIES:
Shadowing Stella
Implicating Claudia
Chasing Sofie (coming soon)

THE LAWKEEPER SERIES:
Lawfully Held
A K-9 LAWKEEPER ROMANCE
Lawfully Taken
A BOUNTY HUNTER LAWKEEPER ROMANCE
Lawfully Defended
A S.W.A.T. Lawkeeper Romance
Lawfully Given
A CHRISTMAS LAWKEEPER ROMANCE
Lawfully Promised
A TEXAS RANGER LAWKEEPER ROMANCE

THE BLUSHING BRIDES SERIES:
The Billionaire's Reluctant Bride
(Releases April 4, 2019)

Standalone novellas:
Holly's Noel

Painting the Sunset Sky (coming soon)

Implicating Claudia

Elle E. Kay

FAITH WRITES PUBLISHING

Benton, Pennsylvania

Copyright © 2016 Elle E. Kay
All rights reserved.
No portion of this book may be reproduced in any form without permission
from the publisher, except as permitted by U.S. copyright law.

Faith Writes Publishing
266 Saint Gabriels Rd
Benton, PA 17814

ISBN: 978-0-9994856-0-6

This book is dedicated to my husband, Joe.
Thank you for your patience and love.

Chapter 1

Claudia balanced a brown paper bag of groceries on her hip while she fumbled for the key to Sameer's off-campus apartment. The two-and-a-half-hour drive from the Carlisle Barracks back to Legion University had left her shoulders tense. Looking down at her Marine Corps uniform, she realized she needed to shower before she started cooking. Her favorite dress was in her backpack. He would be so surprised when he got home and found a romantic dinner waiting for him. She couldn't believe her luck at getting dismissed early from drill on the anniversary of her and Sameer's first date. Smiling, she turned the key in the lock. This would be a magical night. She pushed the door open and hustled inside.

The groceries fell to the floor with a crash. Blood rushed from her face. She grew cold. The odor of scallops and shrimp filled the air as the plastic containers of seafood burst open on the hardwood floor. She sucked in a breath. The other woman shrieked, tried to cover her exposed flesh, and darted toward the bedroom. *Judy. No way.*

Sameer gasped when he met Claudia's gaze. He rubbed his hand across his forehead and turned away. She turned on her heel and walked out, shutting the door behind her. It was happening again.

Judy. Man-thieving little tramp.

Claudia gripped the railing as she stumbled down the stairs. When she reached the landing, she bent over and waited for the wave of nausea to pass. There was nothing to say. No possible justification.

She made it to her car. As she turned the key in the ignition, Sameer tore down the stairs. At least he'd bothered to put on sweatpants. The betrayal stung. Should she get out and confront him? No, he's not worth it. Staring, ahead at the outline of the mountains in the darkening sky, she pressed her foot to the accelerator.

Claudia hurried across the quad. Two bluebirds fluttered past her, a sure sign spring was around the corner. She envied their freedom. The expansive lawns of the campus were still blanketed with snow. She flipped up the collar on her coat and lowered her head to block the wind.

As she approached her car, she saw Sameer. He'd parked near her and was leaning against his car smoking and talking on his cell phone. Lowering her head so he wouldn't know she'd seen him, she hurried past him. He grabbed her by the arm and spun her back to face him. She could taste bile. Glaring at him, she snatched her arm free from his grasp.

"Jessie, I'll have to get back to you, okay? Something has come up." Sameer clicked off his phone and slid it into his back pocket.

Claudia pulled away from him and stepped out of his reach. "What do you mean something has come up? Nothing has come up. I'm leaving." She placed her glove-clad hands on her hips.

"You know I didn't mean for it to happen. Didn't you get my message saying how sorry I was? I thought you Christians were supposed to be forgiving. Why are you being so unreasonable?" He stepped toward her.

Claudia pushed him hard in the chest. "Seriously? Fine. You're forgiven. Is that what you want?"

"No. I want you to let me take you out tonight?" He drew out the words.

"Not a chance. I'm not looking for a repeat performance."

"Aw, come on, it's not like that. It was a one-time thing. A mistake."

"Are you that arrogant? I don't have time for this. Get out of my way."

"Tomorrow? Lunch?" He flashed that crooked smile she was crazy about. The assault on her defenses was too much. She wasn't ready to forgive him, but did she want to walk away? She needed more time to adjust to the idea of losing him. Why hadn't she listened to her father? He'd warned her about dating Sameer.

"I have break at one-twenty. Meet me in the cafeteria," she said.

"Can't we go off campus?"

"No."

"Okay. I'll see you tomorrow." He leaned down to kiss her forehead, but she stepped back. He moved aside, and she pushed past him, kicking at bits of ice. What was she thinking agreeing to see him?

Claudia got into her second-hand Volkswagen beetle. The sun beat on her windshield, enveloping her in warmth. She took off her gloves, pulled her scarf free from her neck, put the blue bug into reverse and backed out of the parking spot. As she drove to her sister's house, thoughts of Sameer filled her head. Part of her wanted to stay with him, but she wouldn't. He was insufferable at times. Thought he knew more than everyone else. But he'd been there for her when she'd needed him.

Why did it have to be Judy? Judy had been her best friend until ninth grade when she'd kissed Claudia's crush. It was only two days ago when she'd let herself into Sameer's apartment that she'd given the girl much thought. As she approached Edinsville, Claudia shook her head, forced her breathing to calm, and reminded herself she was here to spend time with family, not to stew over Sameer and Judy.

She parked in Stella's long driveway and took a deep breath of fresh farm air. Horses dotted the fields and she could see the steeple on her father's church off in the distance.

As she walked toward the front door, a tiny tornado bounded toward her and wrapped himself around her legs. Grinning, she bent down and scooped up the toddler. Stella stood on the porch with an infant on each hip.

Claudia took note of Stella's disheveled appearance and the dark circles under her eyes. She joined her on the porch.

"Hey."

"I'm glad you could come by for dinner. I'm in desperate need of adult conversation."

"You look like you could use help. Jason around?"

Stella shook her head. "Working, as usual."

"Mommy, can Aunt Cwaudia watch *Shrek* with me?" Glen asked in his sweetest voice.

"We'll put it on after dinner, but Mommy and Aunt Claudia are going to talk in the kitchen while you watch it, okay?"

"But Mooommmy, Aunt Cwaudia never gets to watch *Shrek*!"

"I said no." Stella turned and walked back inside. Following her, Claudia deposited Glen into his booster seat at the kitchen table. He sat with his little fists bunched up and an angry scowl on his face. Claudia had to stifle a grin. She took one of the twins from her sister and got to work strapping the little one into his high chair, while her sister did the same for the other one.

"I thought we'd feed the kids first and then we could eat in relative peace." Stella placed macaroni and cheese and diced hot dogs in front of Glen.

"Sounds like a plan." Claudia took one of the proffered jars of baby food from her sister. Claudia fed Cole while Stella fed Paul. Little Cole had a shock of black hair on his head, while his twin brother had a light red peach fuzz.

The kitchen opened out into the living room. It was an ideal floor plan for her sister, allowing her to keep an eye on everything while she worked in the kitchen and the kids played a few feet away.

"How was drill? Did you qualify on the range?"

"Of course. I did well at PT too. The commanding officer dismissed us early on Sunday. I'm sure she had somewhere to be, but I wasn't complaining." No sense in elaborating while they were feeding the kids.

Cole turned his head away from the spoon. After a couple more attempts at getting more food into him, she put the lid back on the jar.

Stella took a baby wipe to three little faces. Then she led the toddler to a miniature recliner beside the couch. "Okay now, Glen, you sit here and watch *Shrek* with your brothers while Aunt Claudia and I have our dinner, okay?"

"Awright. But can Aunt Cwaudia watch it when she's done her dinner?"

"Maybe."

Claudia had followed Stella into the room with a child on each hip. "Put them in here." Stella indicated the pack-n-play.

After getting the twins settled, Claudia made her way back into the kitchen and set the table while Stella pulled the baked ziti from the oven.

Claudia rearranged the food on her plate. She should talk to Stella. She was a good listener, but she didn't need any added stress.

Ten minutes into the meal, Stella pushed her plate away and turned to Claudia. "What's going on with you? You seem distant and you're barely eating."

"It's Sameer."

"Yeah? How is he?"

"Oh, he's fine. A little too fine."

"Spill it."

"I stopped by his apartment the other night and let myself in. I thought he was serious about me when he gave me the key. I found out how wrong I was."

"Why, what happened?"

"Judy was at his place."

"Judy who?"

"Morrow."

"That girl who stole your boyfriend freshman year?"

"Yes, that Judy. But he wasn't my boyfriend. I had a crush on him."

"What was his name?"

"Steven. He and Judy are still together as far as I know. Last I heard, he was stationed in Kuwait."

"What was she doing at Sameer's place?"

"You don't want to hear the details. Suffice it to say, I caught them in the act."

"Wow. How did they end up hooking up?"

"I don't have a clue. I knew she attended Legion when I transferred from community college. I've seen her around campus a few times. This was the first time I saw them together."

"What was Sameer thinking?"

"That's just it." Claudia picked at her perfectly manicured nails. "I think when I made the decision not to have sex again until I was married, it cost me my relationship with Sameer. How can I expect him to understand that I was willing to have sex with previous boyfriends, but not with him? It's only natural that if I won't do it, he'll find someone who will."

"No, that is not 'only natural'. You know waiting until you're married is honorable. You're following your conscience. You can't let Sameer's weakness change your conviction. You're too smart to believe what you just said."

"I don't know what I believe."

"I still can't believe he cheated on you. What an idiot."

"I thought he loved me. Why did he have to jump into bed, well, couch, more precisely, with Judy? Did it *have* to be her?"

"I'm sorry, Claud. You don't deserve this."

"Maybe it's payback for my wild high school days."

"Stop it! That's ridiculous. I don't understand why he would do this, but I know you deserve to have a man who will treat you like a princess." She put her hand over Claudia's. "I liked Sameer, I did. But I hope you aren't going to keep seeing him after this."

"I don't think I can. I agreed to lunch at the cafeteria tomorrow to talk, but I can't see myself continuing a relationship with a guy who would fool around on me."

"I wonder what Steven will do? I hope for Sameer's sake he doesn't find out about this."

"I almost hope he does, but I won't be the one to tell him." Steven wasn't the type to quietly move on. He'd make sure they both paid for their transgression. A certain pleasure came with the thought. But then again, she still loved Sameer. Did she truly want Steven to get a hold of him? Of course not.

"Well, I think it's an ice cream night, don't you? Forbidden chocolate or moose tracks?" Stella opened the freezer door.

"Don't you have any strawberry?"

"No, but I have strawberry syrup and vanilla ice cream."

"Sold. I shouldn't be eating junk. PT doesn't get easier when I stuff my face with garbage."

Stella scooped the ice cream while Claudia rinsed their plates and stuck them in the dishwasher. "Everything in moderation. You don't have drill again for a month."

Claudia rolled her shoulders to get the kinks out. Leaning back on the couch, she shut her eyes for a moment. It had taken an hour to get the children settled and she was worn out.

"You can't keep your eyes open. Why don't you crash in the guest room?" Stella asked. "I'll call Mom and Dad and let them know you're staying here tonight."

"Wouldn't it make more sense to call my roommate? Sofie's the one that'll be expecting me. I'll shoot her a text."

"I can't get used to you not living home with Mom and Dad."

"It wouldn't exactly be practical for me to live home and drive to and from campus every day."

Stella placed her hands on her hips. "I know, but I don't have to like it."

"Your baby sister is a Marine not a Barbie doll. I can take care of myself. Stop worrying."

"I always thought of you more as the Barbie doll type. I still can't believe you joined the Reserves. I'd have been less surprised if you had joined the circus."

"I think I'm going to crash. I need to have my wits about me when I see Sameer tomorrow."

"I don't know why you're bothering to see him. He doesn't deserve the opportunity to explain. You could always cancel or stand him up."

Stella was right, of course. Yet, this was something she needed to do. "Thanks for listening," she headed toward the stairs, "I'll see you in the morning, Sis."

Sameer was waiting at a table in the cafeteria when Claudia strolled in. He tapped his foot as she approached. "You're late."

"I'm here," she slid into the seat across from him.

Sameer grinned. "So, I was thinking, we should put this whole ugly episode behind us and move on. How does that sound?" His raised his brows.

She flicked a piece of invisible lint off of the arm of her cashmere sweater. "It sounds like you're smoking something stronger than tobacco if you think for a minute I would demean myself enough to pretend your escapade with Judy didn't happen."

"Well, what did you expect would happen? I've been asking you for two years to take our relationship to the next level physically. Honestly, how long do you think a man can hold out?"

"Wait, you're blaming me for your infidelity? I expected you to hold out until we were married. I know, it's old-fashioned, but you knew I wanted to wait. How long have you been unfaithful? How many women?" Her voice was too loud. People were staring.

"I thought you would change your mind when we got serious, but come on, enough is enough. Judy wanted attention, I gave it to her. I didn't see the harm. There weren't any others."

"Wow. Unbelievable. How could you not see that your actions would hurt me, not to mention Judy's boyfriend? And, if I were to wager money, I'd put it on you having been unfaithful before her." Standing, she knocked over the chair. "See ya."

"Look, I'm sorry," he slipped to his knees and put his hands in a prayer position, "please don't make me beg."

"Don't bother."

He stood. "Come on, you can't seriously be walking away because of one little fling, can you?"

"Goodbye, Sameer." She stormed from the cafeteria.

"I'm not the sort of guy you can walk away from."

Chapter 2

awson gathered up wood, pulling pieces out from under the layer of snow. He knew how difficult it would be to get the wet wood to burn, but he would need heat in the old house. There were minor repairs he'd promised to make and there was no reason to freeze in the process. He used the path in the woods that led back to the main farmhouse and let himself in the back door which led to the kitchen.

He continued on to the huge living area and loaded up the fireplace with wood and tucked paper and kindling around it, which he found in a metal can kept off to the side of the fireplace. He rubbed his arms to ward off the chill. It felt warmer outside than it did in the house. Once he got the fire started, he made his way back to the kitchen and picked up the telephone.

"Hello. You've reached the office of Pastor Jim McIntyre. Please leave a message at the tone."

"Hey Jim. It's Dawson. I came out to check on the house and noticed strange tire tracks. Thought you should know about them. I'll be around a while and will let you know if anything else seems amiss. Give me a call when you get this message. I'll be in the basement working on the furnace, so if I don't hear it ringing, try again."

Dawson walked back to the front of the house and stared out the bay windows at those fresh tire tracks in the snow. Somebody had been here, but who? And why?

Claudia peered out the window in the loft over the detached garage of her grandfather's house. Someone had been out there. Impressions in the snow appeared to come from the woods and wind around to the stables. Who had been left them? The driveway was a quarter mile long, it wasn't usual for people to wander onto the property. Maybe she should go outside, follow the footprints, and find out where they led. Dismissing the thought, she walked back to her bed. She sat up against the headboard and opened her laptop.

Determined to put the footprints from her mind she clicked on her email for a distraction. She deleted the obvious junk mail first, no she didn't need a cruise vacation or any kind of pharmaceutical miracle drug. She answered a personal email from her roommate, Sofie.

> *Yes, Sofie, I got here okay. Sorry I didn't call; no cell*
> *service and I didn't want to make the trek over in*
> *the snow to the main house. Forgive me. Love ya.*

She clicked on an email from an email address she didn't recognize. The subject line read *Die.* She hovered over delete, but noticed it had a link to a video. Curiosity got the better of her and she clicked it. She grew still and her heart beat rapidly. Her hands shook on the mouse as she recognized her car pulling into the driveway. The video cut to her standing in the window. She rose and slammed the mouse down on the bed. Would Sameer do this? She reached for her cell phone. No service. She opened a browser to connect to Facebook, but it wasn't working. That was odd. She'd been connected a moment ago. She pushed the anxiety down and tried again. It wasn't unusual for Wi-Fi to be lousy out here in the country. There was a landline in the farmhouse.

Her mind was flooded with images of her sister stuck in a cold damp mine with bats shrieking. She hadn't been inside the mine herself, but the descriptions she'd heard from Stella and Jason were enough to form a vivid picture. Why had that popped into her head? It was just a video and footprints. No stalker. Sameer was doubtless getting payback. Trying to scare her. No big deal. She'd joined the Marines, so she would never be a victim.

Grabbing her purse, she headed for the door. With one hand on the butt of her Bodyguard, she trudged across the lawn to the back of the farmhouse, alert. The house was unusually warm when she entered by the back door. Walking slowly toward the living room with her pistol drawn, she encountered the back of a man staring out the big front windows. She racked the slide on her 380.

An unmistakable metallic sound caught Dawson by surprise. He slowly turned from the front window. Staring into the barrel of a gun, he started to raise his arms. Then he recognized the brilliant-blue eyes of the ticked-off young lady wielding it.

"Claudia."

"Dawson." They spoke simultaneously.

"Could you lower the gun?"

She complied. "What are you doing here?"

"Your father asked me to come by and check on the place. He also wanted me to take a look at the furnace and fix the weather-stripping around the door. So, the real question is, what are you doing here?"

"I wanted to get away from school for the weekend."

"Ah. Your dad must've forgotten to let me know you'd be here. Nice gun. M&P?" Dawson held his hand out and Claudia started to hand him the weapon but stopped herself. She pulled out the magazine, emptied the chamber, and then handed him the pistol.

"Yeah, it's a Smith & Wesson M&P Bodyguard."

"Why was it pointed at me?"

"It's a long story. Were those your prints in the snow from the stables to the woods?"

"Yes, they were. My truck is behind the stables."

"Makes sense."

"Come on into the kitchen. If you promise not to draw your weapon, I'll make you something to eat. The house is short on supplies, but I can whip something up."

About twenty minutes later, he served up a pancake breakfast with hot apple topping.

"So, when did my dad start treating you as his personal handyman?"

Dawson laughed. "I don't think he's treating me like a handyman as much as like the kid next door. He forgets I'm a grown man, but it's fine. I enjoy the diversion." She was quite the diversion, too.

Claudia stared at the words in the textbook she was reading, but they weren't registering. Her mind was on her encounter this morning with Dawson. She'd pulled her weapon. Nothing could've prepared her for the reaction she'd gotten. She had seen his handsome face when he turned around. She'd never forget the look on it when he realized it was her holding the pistol. He'd been amused. How could a man be amused when they are staring down the barrel of a gun? If the threat was real, she would have held her own. Her commanding officer would have her head if he'd known she came that close to handing someone a loaded firearm.

She'd been so relieved the footprints were Dawson's. Yet, it bugged her that the video was shot from here. He wouldn't do something so out of character. Not even as a joke. Besides, his surprise at seeing her had been evident. She hadn't told him about the video? Was she afraid he would think her a silly girl who couldn't take care of herself? It's not as if she suspected him, but she didn't plan to go next door and cry on his shoulder.

Her thoughts turned to Dawson's deep brown eyes with those thick lashes. She'd kill for eyelashes like that. She wouldn't need mascara. He had rugged sexy looks. Not her usual type. She was attracted to guys like Sameer. Dawson was distinctive. Attractive, but not in a pretty-boy way. She'd learned her lesson about good-looking men.

It was best to keep your distance from them. She thought back to the nights when they were young, and Stella would talk incessantly about Dawson. Stella's childhood crush was forever ago. Claudia had always thought him attractive, but today it felt like he saw her differently. Probably her imagination.

Should she explore her feelings further, or run in the other direction? Running might be the wise thing to do. After all, she was still hurting over the break-up with Sameer. She didn't need to get involved with another man so soon. Besides, he likely thought of her as a child, at best a niece, at worst a little sister. No way did she stand a chance of getting Dawson Montgomery to notice her.

A noise got her attention. Maybe Dawson had returned? She peeked out the window to see if she saw his truck anywhere, but she didn't. Maybe he'd parked on the other side of the stables again. Then again, sometimes houses just made strange noises. She dismissed her concern about the noise and stared down at her textbook.

Dawson placed the log on the tree stump and lifted the axe over his head bringing it back down with enough force to split it. He shrugged out of his coat and tossed it on the pile of wood. Over and over his encounter with Claudia repeated itself in his head. His thoughts turned to her as a child. She'd been a precocious girl who meandered around the stables, getting in the way. He'd taught her how to ride a horse and just as importantly how to fall. The little girl who had dressed up as a princess, with a tiara on her head, was no longer playing make believe. He'd watched her grow from a tiny child riding her first pony to a teenager riding away alone to sulk.

The Claudia he'd seen today was not that same girl. Nor was she a sulky teen. This Claudia was a fully-grown woman capable of protecting herself. He still couldn't believe she'd pulled a gun on him. Wow. She was dangerously grown up and he would be smart to stay out of her way. He didn't know what to make of this new Claudia. Might as well stick around and help out at the McIntyre farm over the next few days. He'd spend time getting to know this grown-up version of Claudia, even if it was a bad idea.

He thought back to her childhood shenanigans and remembered her trips to his fort in the woods. He'd ignored her and her sister back then. He'd hung out with his own friends, but this young woman was not the kind he could easily ignore. No. He should avoid her much the same as he avoided mushrooms and liver, but every particle in his body told him to ignore common sense and chase after her.

Chapter 3

Claudia drove along Route 220 away from Dushore and toward the town of Laporte. She'd decided to take a drive to clear her head. She considered pulling over and taking a walk on the Loyalsock trail, but the idea of hiking uphill didn't appeal to her, so she kept driving. Another minute or two down the road she heard the telltale sound of a tire going flat. Great. She would have to pull over on the deserted highway and change a flat. She wasn't the get-your-hands-dirty type. She pulled over and popped the trunk.

Wrestling the donut out of the trunk she muttered to herself. "So much for a nice relaxing drive."

Her dad had been hounding her to switch the donut out for a real tire, so she wouldn't have to worry about driving far. Guess the 'I told you so' speech would be coming.

She'd thought a drive at dusk watching the sunset was what she needed to clear her head, but it had not been pleasant so far. She took a blanket from the car and spread it out. Kneeling down, she tried to get the lug nuts loose. They wouldn't budge. Not a weakling by any means, she was in top physical shape not only from her Marine training, but from regular morning runs and weight training. She stood and stomped on the lug wrench hoping to use her leg strength to loosen the nut. It worked. She got one loose, she moved to the next one and repeated the process, until she had them all loose. As she was pulling the tire off the car, a truck pulled in behind her. She waved off the driver before realizing it was Dawson. He ignored her and jumped from his truck.

"How did you know I was out here?"

"I planted a GPS tracking device on your car."

"You did what?"

"Relax, I was joking. I didn't know you were here. In fact, I pulled over to help the stranger on the side of the road before I realized it was you."

"What were you coming this way for?"

"It's the only road out of town in this direction. I was headed over to a buddy's house, but I think he'll understand if I don't show up. I'll call him when we get back. I'm not leaving you to ride on a donut back to the farm by yourself. I'll follow you, then you can hop into my truck and I'll take you out to dinner. I'll bet you haven't been to the Whistle Stop in ages."

"Aren't they closed?"

"I don't know. We'll take a drive into town, and if they're closed we'll go somewhere else."

"Well, if they're not closed, they close early, so how about we stop on our way through town instead of coming back?"

"Anything to keep you from having to get into my truck, huh? Don't want to be in close proximity to me?"

"Don't be silly."

"I don't know. First you pull a gun on me, and now you don't want to get into my vehicle. A guy might develop a complex around you."

Claudia laughed and stepped out of the way, making a grand gesture of turning over the job to Dawson.

"Oh, I'm good enough to change the tire though, huh?"

"Most certainly. You are the proverbial knight in shining armor."

"Lucky me." He leaned down to inspect the tire more closely. "This is strange."

"What is?"

"It looks like your tire was damaged and then filled with Fix-A-Flat. It's not a permanent solution. You either need to take the tire to the pros for a repair or get a new tire."

"I didn't know the tire was damaged."

"Did you lend your car to a friend?"

"No. I have no idea how my tire was damaged. Are you sure?"

"Yes. I'm sure. Look here." He indicated what he was talking about and she nodded, pretending to see what he saw. "I guess you have a mystery on your hands."

He made short work of attaching the donut and putting the flat tire in her trunk. He held her driver's door open for her to climb in. "I'll be right behind you."

"Thanks for the warning."

He shut her door and followed her back into town. She spent most of the ride watching him through her rear-view mirror.

After they parked, Dawson walked to Claudia's car and opened the door for her. "I'm perfectly capable of opening my own door."

"Of course you are. I was trying to be a gentleman."

"Well, stop it."

"As you wish, Ma'am. I'll be sure to let you handle all future doors."

To prove his point, he walked through the door of the Whistle Stop instead of allowing her to enter first, and then let the door swing shut behind him. Claudia made a sound of disgust in her throat before following him through the door.

They took their seats, and she narrowed her eyes and glared at him. He grinned. She kicked him under the table.

"Ouch." He reached across the table and pulled her hair. "Now we're even."

She kicked him again. He decided to ignore her this time.

When the waitress finished taking their order, he asked "What have you been studying in school?"

"I got a scholarship for art."

"Interesting. What do you plan to do with a degree in art? Will you teach or do art therapy or something in that vein?"

"No. Those both require a different degree. I'm simply studying art and have no idea how I plan to use it, yet."

"What have you been up to besides school?"

"Joined the Marines. Broke up with a long-term boyfriend. Otherwise, life has been boring."

"You joined the Marines? That doesn't sound boring."

She sipped the glass of iced-tea the waitress had brought. "The Reserves. It's only a weekend a month and a couple of weeks each year. No big deal. How about you?"

"I haven't been as motivated as you. Managing the farm and work. Dad decided it was time for him to retire. He and Mom are planning to get a retirement home in Arizona. They're out west now looking at houses and staying in a rental condo. They want me to put an addition on the farmhouse for them to live in when they come home for the summers." He leaned back and watched her fidget with her straw.

"So, you'll live in the main farmhouse?"

"Yep. I bought the house and property from them, so they'd have enough money to get what they were looking for in Arizona." The waitress set their food down and glanced toward the clock.

"Cool. I'm happy for your parents. They deserve a nice retirement." She dug into her burger like she hadn't eaten in weeks. There was a comfortable silence while they ate.

"What about your parents? What do you think your dad's plans are?" Dawson asked.

"I don't think he even has retirement on his radar. He's got a savings, a 401(k) or something, but it's still at least twenty years down the road for him. I'm not sure he'll ever quit preaching. As long as he's capable of standing upright."

"How was your burger?" he asked.

"Perfect."

He grinned. "Excellent. You want to come back to my place? Watch a movie?"

"I would, but I have class in the morning, so I should be heading back to campus."

"How are you going to drive back with a flat tire? It's not as if you will find an open shop in Dushore on a Sunday."

"I hadn't thought that far ahead."

"I'll give you a lift back to campus tomorrow, get your tire fixed up on Monday and bring you back to your car when you're ready. Okay?"

"I couldn't ask you to do all that. I can call my dad or Jason."

"You didn't ask. I offered. I want to help."

"Then, okay, I guess. I appreciate it. I won't need my car during the week, so if you could pick me up on Friday after my two o'clock class, that would be perfect."

He smiled. "No problem."

She wasn't even gone, and he was already looking forward to seeing her again. What was wrong with him?

Claudia glanced at the clock and realized she should've checked in by now. Her parents were most likely worried sick. She talked to them virtually every day and it had been several days since she last called.

Picking up the old-fashioned corded telephone, she made the call.

"Hello." Her father's voice sounded strained.

"Hi, Dad. Sorry I didn't call sooner."

"I've been calling your cell, but you haven't picked up."

"Sorry. No cell service. I meant to call this morning. I walked over to the main house and ran into Dawson."

"Oh. I meant to tell you he'd be doing work at the house."

"I figured that out."

"Guess so. Sorry."

"I took a drive today, but got a flat tire."

"Is everything okay?"

"Fine. Dawson came to the rescue. He's going to give me a ride back to the apartment tomorrow and get the tire fixed up on Monday."

"Is he there? Can I speak with him?"

"He left."

"Tell him that I can come up and take care of it. He doesn't need to put himself out."

"I told him the same thing, but he wants to help."

"Okay. I guess I'm not needed."

"Of course, you're needed. Just not for a flat tire. I have to finish my homework."

"Let us know when you are safely back at your apartment."

"I'll text Mom."

"That'll work."

"Love you."

"Love you too, sweetie."

Claudia hung up and stared at the receiver.

Claudia heard Dawson pull up and yelled out the window. "I'll be down in one second."

About ten minutes later, she finally walked down the steps of the garage apartment and threw her bag into Dawson's truck.

He opened the door for her and this time she kept her mouth shut. She didn't want to encourage him to slam doors in her face on a regular basis. "What were you doing up there all this time? Preparing for a nuclear war?"

"I was packing my bag."

"It takes you that much time to pack your bag when you've only been here two nights?"

"Yep."

"All righty then." His grin was huge. She wanted to wipe it off his face, but he was her ride. "I'll head on out over toward Williamsport and you can give me specific directions when we get closer, okie dokie?"

"You talk like a hick, Dawson."

"Well thank ya', Ma'am, that is one of the highest compliments you could give an ol' farm boy." She rolled her eyes and leaned back trying to get comfortable for the lengthy ride.

"Thanks for taking me home."

"Aw shucks, Ma'am, you're more than welcome."

"How long are you going to keep doing that?"

"I haven't decided yet. Why don't you distract me by giving me something else to tease you about? Tell me about school."

"Well, as you know, I'm nearing the end of school, but I have no idea what I'm going to do when I grow-up." She made air quotes, but he didn't see her because he was keeping his eyes on the road.

"I must admit, art was a strange choice for a major, but if you got a scholarship, you must have some pretty special talent. I'm sure you'll do something great with it."

"What do you do these days? Besides running the farm, I mean."

"I'm a computer programmer."

"Where did you find that sort of job in Dushore?"

"I didn't. I work from home. I'm a freelancer. It pays the bills."

"Well, judging by the truck, you're not doing too bad."

"For all you know, I'm in debt up to my eyeballs from buying this truck. Or maybe it was purchased by my dad."

"Your dad isn't the kind of guy to buy his son an expensive truck, so that option is out. And for some reason, you don't strike me as the debtor type."

"We are all debtors, princess. Haven't you read the good book lately?"

Claudia gave him a tiny smile, but didn't answer. He sounded like her father.

A flash of something caught her eye and Dawson quickly swerved the truck off the road onto the shoulder. Her seatbelt tightened. A scream stuck in her throat.

"What was that?"

"A family of raccoons. Don't worry, we didn't hit them. Look." He pointed at the raccoons safely on the other side of the road.

"You almost killed us to save rodents?"

"First of all, they aren't rodents. They're mammals, actually part of the bear family."

"You're lecturing me about species after you come close to killing me?"

"Stop being so dramatic. It's not like you were in any danger. I might've pulled over faster than I would've liked, but we didn't run over the little guys."

She was glad they hadn't hurt the raccoons, but wondered about Dawson Montgomery. The big tough guy with a soft spot for wildlife.

"Now, if it had been a deer, we might have hit it. That would've made for more than a few good dinners."

With those two sentences, he ruined the gentle image she'd formed of him.

Chapter 4

awson arrived in Williamsport earlier than necessary. He hadn't been to town for a while and thought he might walk around and find something to do while he waited for Claudia to finish her last class. As he ambled down the street, he let his mind wander. He considered his options with her. Most likely, she wasn't interested in him as more than a big brother sort. He'd been a part of her life for so long, he was like the furniture. Comfortable. Reliable. But not exciting and entertaining.

He considered his newfound interest in Claudia; she was exquisite, a work of art. He thought it was strange he hadn't noticed before. Sure he'd thought she was cute, and she always had an unusual beauty, something fascinating that he couldn't put into words, but he'd never had an interest in her. She was too young. Too innocent. There was nothing naive or innocent about the woman who had pulled her pistol on him.

Nothing caught his interest on the streets of Williamsport, so he headed back toward Claudia's apartment and settled down on her steps to wait for her. It wasn't long until she appeared off in the distance walking with a man at least twice her age. They were engaged in deep conversation. She was so enthralled with him she didn't notice Dawson sitting there until the man introduced himself. "Professor Marcus. And you are?"

"Dawson Montgomery. A friend of Claudia's."

"Nice to meet you, Mr. Montgomery. Claudia, I'll see you in class on Monday. Enjoy your weekend."

"A little cozy with the professor, interesting." He raised an eyebrow. He wasn't going to let her know it bothered him in the slightest.

"Stuff it." She punched him in the arm.

"I just noticed something," Dawson said.

"Don't say it."

"Claudia McIntyre has a naked face. You didn't put on any makeup this morning. I don't think I've seen you without it since you were thirteen years old, sneaking around to put it on without your parents noticing."

"Leave it alone. My hives were bothering me, so I didn't think I should wear it today."

"I don't see any hives."

"That's because I didn't wear my makeup."

"Interesting. Had I not arrived before you had a chance to go inside, would I have been privileged enough to see you without a painted face?"

"Not likely."

"Well, I'll give you a few minutes to get ready, but I recommend you leave off the war paint."

Claudia rolled her eyes as she unlocked the apartment door. He grabbed the door and held it for her to enter ahead of him.

"Don't get on my nerves today."

"Oh, I remember now. I'm supposed to let the door slam on you, so you can be a strong, independent feminist."

"Shove it."

He grinned.

"Grab a water or something for yourself while I run upstairs and get ready."

He took her up on the offer and grabbed a water from her refrigerator. She wasn't eating well here. It was stocked with nothing but water, soda, and a couple of expired yogurts. He would make sure she got a decent meal tonight. He was thinking they could grill up steaks. He'd taken a couple out of the freezer. He might be able to round up some broccoli or something to satisfy her need for vegetables.

Claudia was only upstairs for fifteen minutes, but it felt longer. Disappointment filled him when he saw she had indeed put on makeup while she was upstairs.

"Why?" he asked.

"Why what?"

"You know what."

"Because I feel naked without it. I had to put a little on. Mascara and lipstick."

"You don't need the stuff."

"Whatever. Are you ready to go?"

"I've been waiting on you. Want to share some steak with me tonight?"

"You don't have to feed me. I'm sure there is food over at Pop's house."

"There isn't much over there. Remember I made the pancakes the other day. There were a few jars of canned fruit and veggies. That's it. Besides, I'd like to feed you. I see you've been eating like a bird around here."

"I eat out a lot."

"I'll make you a nice home-cooked meal. You won't regret it. I promise."

"Said the fox to the hen before he devoured her."

"I'm no fox, but I'm glad you appreciate me," Dawson said.

"You went there?"

"I did. So, do you want to have steak with me tonight?"

"I guess."

"An enthusiastic yes if I ever heard one. Let's go."

Claudia was surprised at the change in the house. What had been a homey colonial house, had been renovated to a modern masculine one. The scent of the leather furniture filled the living room. The tables were glass. There was no longer an antique scarred wood table made of sturdy construction filling the dining room. It had been replaced with a baby grand piano. She ran her fingertips across it as she walked by. Across the room from the piano was a black desk with both a desktop computer and Dawson's laptop. Everything was meticulous. Not a pen out of place.

Claudia made an odd sound in her throat. It was Dawson's turn to raise an eyebrow. "Something wrong?"

"Of course not, but I didn't expect such a considerable change in the house."

"Don't you like it?"

"It's great. But, I hadn't expected it. It could use a feminine touch, I think."

"Are you volunteering for the job?"

Claudia bit her lip. "No. I'm not."

The steak was juicy and tender. Claudia savored every bite. The sun was setting. Dawson had set the table with linen napkins and fancy china. He'd lit a fire in the big stone fireplace. The sun was setting, but she could still see the cows that grazed in the fields and the mountains off in the distance.

"I'm surprised you made steamed broccoli and cauliflower. I expected baked potatoes or something equally masculine."

"Do I look like a savage?"

"A little. Yes." She smiled.

Dawson's hearty chuckle filled the space between them. "I guess if I wasn't having company, I wouldn't have stopped on the way to pick up vegetables. I would've only cooked a baked potato. Speaking of which, I left them in the microwave. The company may have had something to do with the short-term memory loss."

"Ha. I knew there would be baked potatoes! Or microwaved potatoes as the case may be."

The look in his eyes intensified. "It's a beautiful night to spend with such a beautiful woman."

"What are you buttering me up for? Have a kitchen in need of scrubbing?"

"Can't a man say something nice to a lady without having an ulterior motive?"

"Not in my experience. No."

"You must have rather limited experience."

She choked on her water. Instead of responding, she cleared the dishes and carried them to the sink. "Thanks for dinner and for taking care of my car issues. I owe you several favors."

"No, you don't. We'll call it even since you agreed to have dinner with me. It was nice to have company."

"I'm going to head next door and get my homework started."

"Let me grab my keys. I'll drive you over."

"I can walk the trail. It's no big deal."

"I don't want you walking over there in the dark. There are bear in them there woods."

"Okay." A heavy sigh escaped. "I'll take a ride." She enjoyed the night air and the sounds of the woods, but he had a legitimate point. She should accept the ride. Especially after the weird events of last weekend.

They were back at her place in less than two minutes. "You want to come in for a cup of hot cocoa?"

"Absolutely."

He sat at the kitchen table while she made the cocoa. She'd been surprised he'd agreed to come in. She thought he would've wanted to get home. Although, he must not see many people during the week, working from home and always hanging out on the farm. Maybe he was bored. She wouldn't read too much into his presence.

It was a brand-new day and Dawson planned to make the most of it. He'd enjoyed spending time with Claudia last night, but he found himself in a real dilemma. Did he pursue her and put their families' relationships at risk? Praying about it hadn't shed any light on the situation. Yet. Was he only interested in her because she was beautiful? Or was there more to his sudden infatuation?

Most certainly there was more to it, wasn't there? He'd known her his entire life. Yes, she was gorgeous, but he hadn't been drawn to her before. There was something unfamiliar about her and it was captivating him. He couldn't put his finger on what it was. She'd always been gutsy. Always had a spark of rebellion and fire. This was different. There was a calm self-assurance, not pridefulness, but an awareness of herself. He wanted to see more of it.

He stood on the front porch and gazed in the direction of her family's farm. He couldn't see it through the woods, but knowing she was so close, gave him a strange measure of comfort. He had work to get done, so he headed in and got down to it. It was a productive morning, and by noon he'd made a huge dent in his work load and was ready for some playtime. Had she finished her homework? Was she ready for a break? Maybe they could take the horses out. She loved to ride. They still had a couple of hours before the sun went down.

A few minutes later he was knocking on her front door.

"I thought I heard a car pull up," she said.

"Not exactly a car." He glanced over at the pick-up.

"What's up?"

"I was wondering if you finished your homework."

"Why?"

"Because I'm going to take one of the horses out. I thought you might be interested in joining me."

"I haven't finished my homework, but I could delay it for a few hours. Let me throw on jeans and boots." She looked down at her cotton slacks and angora sweater. "I don't think I'm dressed for horseback riding."

"I think you're right. Why are you dressed up?"

"I'm not dressed up. I'm simply not dressed down."

"You talk in riddles."

Before long she was pulling the door shut behind her and climbing into his pick-up.

"You can ride Snowflake. She's always liked you."

"She must be getting old."

"Hush. She still thinks she's young. She's only twelve, after all."

"Wow. It seems like she's been around longer."

Dawson mounted Huckleberry. "Which path do you want to take? Down by the pond?"

"Sounds great. If you'd given me more of a warning, I would've prepared a picnic dinner for us."

"We can grab burgers in town if you're still up for eating when we get back."

"I wasn't looking for an invitation to dinner. I still have homework to finish, remember?"

"It'll be nice to have someone to eat with. You can do your homework after."

Claudia enjoyed the nice pace he set. It was a peaceful afternoon. Gunshots broke the silence, but she didn't flinch. It wasn't unusual to hear gunshots out here. "It's strange. If there were gunshots in Williamsport, I'd be taking cover. Here it's nothing."

Dawson laughed.

As they neared the pond, he slowed. Claudia quickly dismounted, not wanting him to offer his help. He jumped down and put his hand out for the reins. "How was she for you?"

"Her usual sweet self. I'm sure I'll be feeling the ride tomorrow. It's been a while since I've ridden."

"You should make the time. Your horse presumably misses you when you don't get home to Edinsville."

"Yes, Ava is always happy to go for a ride, but Mom takes her out when I'm not around. She doesn't stay cooped up."

"I'm sure you'd prefer to take her out yourself." He let the horses graze and looked back toward Claudia.

"Someday, I hope I can find work that will allow me to live in the country. I don't know if it will happen, though. I used to think city life would be glamorous, but not anymore. Don't get me wrong, I still like to spend time in the city, the constant commotion and the lights are a real draw for me, but you can't see the stars at night and you can't have a horse." She walked around the pond and he fell in step beside her.

"I never had the slightest desire to spend time in the city. I went to a New Year's party in New York once. I wouldn't do it again," Dawson said.

"Why not? Didn't you have fun?"

"No. It was not fun. My date got plastered and spent the night barfing out the window of my truck. Not a pleasant way to ring in the new year. I spent the following day scrubbing vomit off the paint job."

"But the city has fun stuff to enjoy. Museums, movies, night life. Maybe you could learn to love the city, at least on occasion. Change isn't always a terrible thing, you know. It can lead to greater things if you're open to it."

"I'm open to change, but not when it comes to country versus city. I'm pretty set in my ways."

"You don't think you'll ever live in the city?"

"Not a chance. I need to settle down with a woman who loves the country. A city girl won't do."

"Whoa. When did we start talking about you finding a girl to marry and settle down with? I simply meant you might want to live in the city if a fantastic job opportunity arose."

"I'm happy with the work I have. I enjoy what I do, and I can live where I love. The best of both worlds."

"So, you're completely closed off to the idea of living in the city?"

"Yes. I sure am. Why? Does that bother you, city squirrel?"

"I'm not a squirrel. And I told you already. I changed my mind about living in the city, but I still like spending time there."

"You're prerogative, I suppose." He picked up a rock and skipped it along the water.

"We should think about heading back soon."

"Yes, if we want to get to town by dinner time, we should head back." He rounded up the horses and held the reins while she mounted Snowflake.

Chapter 5

*D*riving into the church parking lot, he surveyed the area. Choosing a spot in the back, out of sight, he parked. There were a few cars in the lot, but the trees and shadows gave him good cover. He hoped the lack of attendance wouldn't mess up his plans. There had to be someone worthy. He'd made up a game for choosing his companions. He liked to choose the fifth to leave the church. Five was the biblical number for death, so could any other number be more fitting?

Not long after he arrived, the pastor held the door and shook hands with each of the attendees as they left the building. He counted as they left. The pastor was number one, the little girl two, and the middle-aged man three. He thought he was out of luck when the fourth person, an older woman exited the building. Was there no number five? Only four people at prayer meeting? But then he noticed there was another younger woman trailing behind her. She'd be perfect. Number five. Always number five.

A fair-skinned, dark-haired beauty.

He waited and watched. *Will they ever stop gabbing?* The two women strayed away from the group and stood outside of a compact car. The door was open, but they weren't making any move to leave. He would wait.

And wait he did. It was more than an hour later when the silver car finally pulled out of the lot. He waited for the older woman to make a left before following the silver car as it turned right. He threw caution to the wind and tailgated her, turning his high beams on so she would be blinded. What a rush knowing her God couldn't help her now.

She sped up, trying to get away from the bright lights, so he increased his speed to stay on her tail. How he would love to give her car a love tap, but he knew it would be too risky. Couldn't leave evidence.

Number five turned into a gas station, in all probability, hoping he would drive on past. He turned on the street past the gas station and drove around the block to come into the station behind her. Walking up to the counter, he asked for a pack of cigarettes. He didn't smoke.

Returning to the vehicle he'd left parked beside the pump, he packed the cigarettes he had no intention of smoking. Watching her return to her car and put on her lip balm, he put his car in gear. He waited for her to start her car and followed her through the streets once more. The town was abuzz with activity. Groups of teen boys on the street with their pants falling off their rear-ends. What a sad state this world was in. He thought back to his own childhood. He'd been well-loved by a godly grandmother, but his allegiance had been to his father. His father had been in prison for as long as he could remember. When he'd visit the prison, his father would tell him to stay out of trouble. Listen to Grandma and stay off the streets. He'd obeyed. Had kept excellent grades all through his school years and went on to get his doctorate. He was intelligent. A better class than these street thugs. They disgusted him. He shook off the thoughts and concentrated on the silver car ahead of him. After she parked her car outside of a pizza shop, she walked inside. Impatiently, he waited for her to emerge from the shop. When she did, he got out of the car and followed her. His prey was on foot this time. He didn't let it deter him. He managed to catch her alone in the alley behind her dorm. Standing there in the secluded alley, she fumbled around in her purse for her keys. She was making this too easy. What was the fun in that? She was startled as he walked up behind her. "Oh, excuse me, Sir. You must have the wrong door."

"No mistake my dear." He covered her mouth with his gloved hand and held a knife to her delicate throat. "You're going to come with me. Understand?"

"Ye-e-es."

"Walk nice and natural back to the pizza shop."

"O-k-k-kay."

"Stop stuttering. I don't have the patience for nonsense."

"So-r-r-ry."

The blade at her neck made the tiniest nick. Enough to let her know he was serious.

As they arrived back at his car, he walked her across to his car and opened the driver's door for her. "Get in. You're driving."

"I "I do-o-on't know how to drive a sti-ick shift."

"Okay, we'll take your car."

He pulled her back out of the car, tugging hard on her hair and taking pleasure in her wince of pain. They walked to her car and he opened the door. The alarm went off. "Turn it off." He made sure the edge of the blade dug into her delicate skin.

She dug the keys from her purse and hit the button on her key fob to disable the alarm.

He forced her into the driver's seat and scooted in behind her before she had a chance to lock the doors or drive away. He leaned forward, holding the knife close to her throat while she drove. He gave her directions to his home. He didn't have to worry about her ratting him out because she wouldn't be leaving there alive.

He entered his cabin and started a fire to take the chill out of the air. It wasn't freezing, but it was close. In the mid-thirties, he believed. He'd left number five outside, but she'd be fine. She was attached to the chain with the handcuffs. He'd used it before. More than once. It always held them. She was a special treasure. How could he have been so lucky to have one that was so lovely? Too bad he wasn't that kind of guy. He wouldn't use her as some men would. She was simply a tool. A means to an end. She would help him to prove the Christian God was a farce. The Christian God couldn't even save the number fives. If he wanted, he could take more of them. It was easy. He was careful, but he didn't have to do much to hide his crimes. Were they crimes? If they brought a great truth to light? Proved to the world there was no God. No greater power pulling everyone's strings like a master puppeteer. Surely, if their God existed, He would prevent the deaths of all the precious number fives.

He turned the outside light on and watched out the window as the girl shook uncontrollably. He could see her lips muttering as she prayed. Yes, she was praying for sure. They all prayed. He sat in the recliner by the window and watched her for hours, not tiring of seeing her shiver, unable to warm herself. After watching her suffering for about three hours, he brought her a blanket. She stared at him with tears in her eyes. He wasn't sure if she was scared or grateful. Maybe both.

He sauntered back inside and continued to watch the show outside his window. He dozed off in his chair. At about four a.m. he awoke. He looked out the window. She appeared to be sleeping. He pitied her. This was the end. He could use his knife, but it would leave too much mess to clean up. He'd tried before. He grabbed a golf club from the bag by the door and crept outside quietly. He lifted the club and used it to put an end to the lovely creature still kneeling with her head down in sleep on his porch. Now her sleep would be permanent.

He unlocked the handcuffs and carried her to his car. Oh no. He left his car at the pizza shop. Her trunk wasn't lined with plastic. He laid her down beside the car and hurried back inside to get plastic to line her trunk. Now he wouldn't have time to take her to a park. He had office hours and didn't want to miss them. That would be suspicious. He arrived at the school with time to spare, so he thought he might as well dump her body. It was as acceptable a place as any. He knew where all the cameras were and there were none by the employee entrance, so he snuck her in that way. He wrapped her body in the plastic from the trunk to keep from dripping blood everywhere and leaving evidence. He had to pass one camera, but was able to use her body to block himself from it.

Once he had her positioned just right on the floor of the art room, he rolled the plastic up and stuffed it in a trash bag. He'd take that with him and burn it. Now to get back to the car and bring it back here quickly, so that there wouldn't be anything tying him to the crime. He'd worn gloves while driving her car, so he should be safe. He smiled to himself. His trunk was still lined with plastic ready for his next adventure.

Claudia grabbed her books off the front seat and headed toward her art class. She hoped to get there in time to catch up with Professor Marcus before class started, so she could ask him a question about an assignment. She was too early, the professor hadn't arrived yet. After hanging her book bag on a hook, she took her sketchbook over to a table.

Sitting down, she opened her book to her assignment before a glint of light caught her attention on the other side of the room. She took a closer look and realized the light had come from the shine off a golf club. *What on earth is that doing in the room? Are we going to draw a golf club?* She was sure the instructor had a brilliant idea of how to use it, but curiosity got the better of her and she hopped from her perch on the stool and walked toward the club. A scream tore from her throat and pierced the silence when she saw the bloodied body of her childhood friend crumbled on the floor beyond the club. She shook Judy's shoulder hoping to wake her. Maybe she'd passed out. Yet, she could clearly see that Judy wasn't going to respond.

The door swung open, and Professor Marcus walked in. "I heard a scream."

Claudia checked for a pulse. "Over here behind the counter."

"Oh my! What have you done, darling?"

"What? I didn't do anything. I came here to talk to you. I found her this way."

"I'm going to call the police. Don't touch anything else. They don't need us tampering with evidence."

Claudia stared at her hands. They were shaking uncontrollably. She hadn't had a chance to forgive Judy. Her heart splintered into thousands of tiny shards. This had been her friend ages ago. She'd loved her. She'd been angry. First Steven and then Sameer. But she'd always believed someday they might be friends again. Now that chance had been torn away. Why? She hadn't done anything so terrible that she deserved to die.

A police officer was lifting her up from her place on the floor. He pulled her hands behind her back and cuffed her. "I didn't do this! Where are you taking me?"

"You have the right to remain silent..."

She stopped listening and retreated to that place inside herself where nobody could hurt her.

"I told you everything I know. Can I go home now?"

"Ma'am, we appreciate your being upfront about your relationship with the deceased, but there are too many holes in your story. We'll be able to pinpoint the time better after the autopsy is complete, but we expect the victim was murdered early this morning. You were found in the classroom with the victim's blood on your hands. You have provided no plausible explanation for why you would bend down and put your hands on the body. I'm afraid you won't be going anywhere for a while. We're going to need to keep you here until we can corroborate your story."

"Am I under arrest?"

"Not yet. Why shake her?"

"I wasn't sure she was dead!"

"So, you shook her?"

"I was shaking her to wake her."

"If you were concerned, why not check her pulse? Isn't that what you've been trained to do?"

"I panicked."

"I'm still not sure I get your presence in the art room that early."

"I was there to talk to my professor."

"He said you didn't have a scheduled appointment."

"I didn't need one. He keeps office hours."

"I see."

"I need to call my father."

"Sure. As soon as I get a few more questions answered."

"Do I need a lawyer?"

"I don't know, do you? Do you have something to hide?"

"No. I'm not guilty, but you're treating me like a suspect."

"You are a suspect."

"Get my father on the phone, so he can get me a lawyer."

Chapter 6

A man wearing wire-rimmed glasses walked into the interrogation room. "Officers. I'd like a moment alone with my client."

"Have at it." One of the officers pushed his chair away from the table with force and slammed out the door.

The younger officer who remained in the room held out his hand to the lawyer. "I'm Officer Gallagher. Officer Jenkins is a little testy. We've been trying to find out what happened for hours and your client is stonewalling us."

"Excellent." The attorney stuffed his hands in his pockets.

Officer Gallagher's smile turned into a scowl. He left the room pulling the door shut behind him.

Peter Keen towered over Claudia and his dark eyes bored through her. "I trust you didn't admit to anything."

Claudia shook her head. "I didn't do anything to admit to. I think you may have upset Officer Gallagher."

"Don't worry about him. Let's talk about this morning. Tell me what happened. Just the big picture."

"Sure. I went into my classroom wanting to meet with the professor to talk about an assignment. I sat down to wait for him to arrive. I noticed a glint on the other side of the room and walked over there only to find Judy's body. I screamed, and Professor Marcus walked in."

"Okay. Did you touch the body?"

"Yes. I tried to shake her to see if she was still alive."

"You shook her? Why?"

"I told you why." Claudia sighed.

"Didn't that seem strange to you? Maybe you should've checked her pulse."

"Now you sound like the cops. I wasn't thinking straight. I did check her pulse after I shook her."

"I doubt the cops have anything to hold you on."

"I didn't do it."

"That's correct. I'll have you out of here in time for dinner. Hold tight for a minute."

Claudia watched as he hurried from the room.

She picked at a hangnail and stopped herself. No sense in ruining her manicure.

The door opened, and Mr. Keen motioned for her to join him in the hall. "You're free to go Ms. McIntyre. Your father is waiting in the reception area. I'm going to get information from these officers, but I'll be in touch first thing in the morning. Avoid the press until then. Use back doors. Don't go out to eat. I'll walk you out to your father's car."

When the doors of the station opened Claudia was pressed by the crowd. A cacophony of voices came at her.

"Did you do it?"

"How did you get released?"

"What do they have on you?"

Her lawyer on one side and her father on the other shielded her from the view of the news cameras. She let out a sigh of relief as they drove from the crowd.

"Dad, this is crazy. Why does everyone think I killed Judy?"

"I don't know. There was mumbling about motive. She was fooling around with your boyfriend."

"You don't think I did it, do you?"

"Of course not. I know you too well. Relax. The police will figure out who did it and then everyone will forget about you."

"I hope they hurry up. They're convinced I'm guilty. Do you think they'll look for anyone else?"

"They will follow where the evidence leads. We both know it won't lead to you. Trust in the Lord."

"I'll try."

"Don't try. Do it."

When they arrived at her parents' house in Edinsville, there were more news vans and reporters waiting for them. Her father kept driving. "Here, take my telephone. Call your mom. Tell her to meet us at the farmhouse in Dushore."

Claudia did as she was told, grateful her father was going to take her to a place of relative peace. She couldn't go back to school and she couldn't go home. She thanked God silently for a safe place to go.

Claudia sat at the big table in the farmhouse. She was sitting beside her father. The table seemed empty with only the two of them. Her father suggested she should stay at the farm until everything calmed down. She'd been here a few weeks ago. Part of her relished the idea of spending more time with Dawson, but on the other hand, what would he think? He might believe her to be guilty. Did he watch the news? She was sure he must.

She put her hand over her father's. "Daddy, you can go home."

"No, sweetie, I can't. It's my responsibility to see to your safety. And I plan to do so."

"I'm a grown woman."

"Maybe the law says you are, but you're still our baby. Your momma will be here soon. I'm sure she'll bring food, so we can have a nice meal together. Let's move into the living room in the meantime and start a fire."

Watching her father lay the wood in the fireplace made her think of Dawson. She hoped he'd come by. He would be able to make her smile. The thought caught her off guard. Since when did she think of Dawson Montgomery in those terms? She needed to get a grip. If only this day would end. Once it was over, she'd be back to her 'in control' self.

She was grateful for the distraction when she heard a car in the driveway. She rushed to the door. Running outside she hugged her mother. Then grabbed a grocery bag and carried it in. "What is all this stuff?"

"Well, I didn't know how long we would be out here, so I stopped by the store. Stella, Jason, and the boys are coming. They are going to stay a few days while we get this all figured out. Stella was going to stop and pick up KFC. It'll be cold by the time she arrives, but we can heat it up in the oven."

"Cold chicken never hurt anyone," Jim said.

Her mom came around the counter after depositing the bag on the round kitchen table. She enveloped Claudia in another hug. The smell of gardenias was comforting. "I'm fine. A little shaken is all," Claudia said.

"You'll be better after you have a meal. Stella won't be long. I'm sure of it. She was going to head out as soon as Jason got home from work. He was on his way home when I spoke to her," Joy said.

"It'll be wonderful to see them."

"Yes, yes it will. Children always brighten up a dark day. Why don't you go up to your room over the garage and get a little rest. You've had a grueling day."

"As appealing as that sounds, I think I'll stay here."

The telephone rang, and her dad reached for it. A moment later he held it out to her. "It's your lawyer."

"Thanks."

"Hello."

"Hi, Ms. McIntyre. I've got great news for you. Security cameras have cleared you. They have footage of a man carrying in the body. He seemed familiar with the locations of the cameras, but he was unable to completely avoid them. It's fuzzy, so they weren't able to identify him, but the image shows someone over six feet tall. No charges have been filed against you, and now you can rest assured they won't be. I'm going to head back to Philadelphia. I don't think they'll be bothering you anymore."

"Thank you." Claudia disconnected the call. "Praise the Lord."

She walked over to her father, a smile forming. "They have footage of the body being carried into the school. They can tell it wasn't me. I'm free. The press should stop bothering me now."

"Oh, honey. I wish it were that simple. I knew you'd be cleared quickly, but the press isn't going to leave you alone. At least not until the next big thing happens. You're still the one who found the body and who was interviewed by the police. Until they arrest someone or something else catches the interest of the press, they'll be camped out on the doorstep. Most likely at your campus apartment and the house in Edinsville. If they find out about this place, then we'll be dealing with them here, as well."

"Oh, please, no. Don't let them come here. I need to be able to breathe."

"I know, sweetie. Something new will happen in a couple of days. It always does. Then you can go home."

"What am I supposed to do in the meantime?"

"Stay here. Dawson's right next door. I can call him and ask him to keep an eye on you."

"I don't need a babysitter."

"I know, but you might enjoy the company. He's a good man. I trust him."

Claudia answered on the first ring.

"Hey, Sofie, what's up?"

"Did you get my text?"

"No service, remember?"

"A package came for you."

"Does it look important?"

"I don't know. It looks as if someone typed your name on the envelope with an old-fashioned typewriter. That seems weird. No return address or postage, so it must've been hand-delivered."

"Did you see who left it?"

"Don't you think I would've mentioned that instead of telling you it didn't have postage?"

"Oh. Duh. Sorry. Can you open the envelope and see who it's from?"

"Sure." There was rustling over the line. "It says 'A gift from the bottom of my heart.' It's made up of cut-out letters from magazines. Like you'd see in a movie or something."

"Are you kidding?"

"What do you think?"

"I suppose not. Can you open the package?"

"I guess. It isn't ticking, so perhaps it's a bad joke. Sameer, maybe?"

"It's possible."

"Here goes. I'm opening it."

"Ouch, you hurt my ear drum. What are you shrieking about?" The crash that followed let Claudia know that Sofie dropped her cell phone.

A few moments later Sofie's voice was back on the line. "It's a heart."

"What do you mean it's a heart? Like a valentine heart or a necklace?"

"No. Like the type that beats in your chest."

"Are you sure?"

"I'm a biology major."

"Are you sure it's not an animal heart, maybe from a deer?"

"I'm almost certain."

"Call the police. I'm with my dad. We'll get there as fast as we can."

"Okay."

"I'm sorry I asked you to open that box for me. It was stupid of me."

"You had no way of knowing what was in it."

"Still. I'm sorry."

"It's okay. I'll only be traumatized, for the rest of my life. It's all your fault."

"I can't believe you're still being a sarcastic jerk."

"It helps me cope. Hurry home, okay?"

"Yep. I'll be there in record time."

Claudia walked into the living room where her father was reading his Bible. Her voice trembled. "Dad, I have to go home. Sofie opened a package that was meant for me. I made the mistake of asking her to open it and see what it was. It had what she thinks is a human heart in it. She's calling the police, but I must go home. I can't leave Sofie to deal with this on her own."

"That is terrible! Let me get packed up and we'll leave immediately."

"You didn't bring much, Dad. We came from the police station."

"We did. I'll grab my keys and my wallet, and we'll get going. What am I thinking? Your mother brought my stuff. I do have a bag. It's upstairs."

"Yes, you're right. Sorry, I'm not thinking clearly."

"Let's get moving. Get your stuff. Meet me at the door in five minutes."

"Okay, Dad."

There was a knock on the door. As her dad reached for it, the telephone rang. Claudia hurried to get the phone. "Hello." She paused and listened to her mother rambling quickly on about an accident one of the deacons was in. He rolled his tractor and had been pinned under it. "I'll get Dad."

She interrupted her father who was talking to Dawson in the hall by the front the door. "Dad, Mom's on the phone. It's important."

"Hi," she said when her dad left to go get the phone."

"Hi. Your dad told me what happened. Are you okay?"

"Yeah. I'm shaken up. That was Mom on the phone."

"I heard that."

"She said Dad's close friend, Joe, rolled his tractor. His daughter, Lydia, went out and found him stuck under the tractor. He's in critical condition. He had to be life-flighted to the hospital."

"Wow. Sounds serious. Now, tell me more about this package your father mentioned."

She told him what she knew.

"Your father can't be in two places at once. I'll go with you to see Sofie. If you want me to?"

"Thank you. I'd appreciate the company."

Jim came back into the room. "You heard what happened. I need to be there, but I need to be with my daughter more."

"I know you want to help me, Dad, but the police will take care of it. It's okay. Dawson said he'd go with me. Go to the hospital. You should be with Joe. I'll call you after we catch up with Sofie."

"Are you sure?"

"Of course," Claudia said.

Jim hurried from the house, kissing her and shaking Dawson's hand on his way out. "Thanks for being there for us. Again."

"I'm glad to help in any way I can."

After her father had left the house, she giggled.

"What are you laughing about?"

"Your timing. You always show up when I need rescuing."

"I forgot my shiny armor, should I go home and change?"

She smiled slightly in response and headed out the door.

Dawson sat beside Claudia and Sofie as they answered questions. He could see that the experience had taken its toll on them. Claudia rubbed her eyes and yawned. Sofie leaned her head back on the couch, resting her eyes.

"Listen, the girls are exhausted. They've been answering questions for hours. Neither of them know anything more than they've already told you. How about we wrap this up, so they can get some rest."

"I'm done with the questions for them, but I actually have a few more for you, Mr.—um, what was your name again?"

"Montgomery. Dawson Montgomery."

"Oh, yeah. We need to establish your time line, clear you from the suspect list."

"Are you serious?"

"As a heart attack."

"Bad joke, don't you think, considering the circumstances?"

The officer tried to hide his face as it turned beet red. "Um. Sorry. It wasn't intentional."

"How about we step outside and get fresh air while we finish up with your questions and let the girls go upstairs and get their stuff. I don't think they're going to want to spend the night here after this incident." Dawson said.

"Sure."

Dawson trudged outside with the officer. He gave account of his whereabouts for the past few days. They didn't have a time of death. The coroner had been called to the scene and confirmed the heart was human, but that was the extent of their knowledge. The box hadn't been in the foyer when Sofie left for film club three hours before she'd returned to find it. That left only a short window of time when the box could've been placed there.

Following the officer's departure, Dawson went back inside and hollered up the steps "Ladies, are you ready yet?"

"I'm not going anywhere," came Sofie's voice, firm in its insistence.

"What do you mean you're not going anywhere? You can't stay here after what happened. What if the guy comes back?" Dawson asked.

"I'm not going anywhere."

"Please come with us." Claudia's voice took on a whiny quality.

"Look, Sofie. This isn't up for debate. I already promised the officer that you two were coming with me, so you're coming with me. Otherwise, I will have to call him back and he may want to put you in protective custody. So, you can come with me, or you can go with him. Your choice."

"Fine. I'll be down in two minutes."

Dawson made the whole thing up about the protective custody, but it was effective.

Chapter 7

They pulled up outside of Dawson's place and Claudia raised her eyebrows. "I thought we were going to my grandfather's place?"

"We don't know if the guy who sent the threatening package knows where your family's place is. We're right next door, of course, but it's one step safer to my way of thinking." He came around and opened the truck door for them.

Claudia and Sofie followed Dawson as he hurried to the door. Claudia peeked over at Sofie. She was still pale and her eyes had a faraway look in them.

"Maybe we should get Sofie something to eat," Claudia said.

"I'm fine. Don't talk about me as if I'm not here."

"Sorry. Do you have food, Dawson?"

"Absolutely. I'll cook something. You guys should relax for a few minutes."

"Where's the bathroom?"

"Down the hall to your left." He pointed the way.

After they left the room, Claudia sat down at the piano. There was a book of sheet music sitting on the piano. It was opened to *It Is Well with My Soul*. How fitting. She had such inner turmoil, but knew if she put her faith in God where it belonged, she could have peace within. She allowed her fingers to find the notes as she lost herself in the music. When she finally glanced up, she found both Sofie and Dawson staring in her direction.

"Beautiful. I didn't know you could play so well," Dawson said.

"I didn't realize you would hear me. Sorry."

"You sounded as lovely as any songbird I've ever heard."

"Stop it, Sofie. You're such a sarcastic brat."

"Yes, I am. But not now. You sounded beautiful. I like hearing you sing while you play. Can you play something else? Maybe something contemporary?"

"I can. I won't. But I can."

"Come on, please. It'll take my mind off everything."

"Let me see what else is in this old song book."

Dawson came up and took the book out of her hand. He pulled one out of a nearby trunk and handed it to her, opening it up to a piano duet for "Peace like a River."

He probably didn't have anything to suit Sofie's taste. He sat close beside her and played. She joined in, enjoying the contact of his leg touching hers on the piano bench.

Sofie walked over and leaned on the piano as they played. She looked better. As if the distance and the music had somehow calmed her. Her forehead was smoothed of the earlier worry lines and she no longer had her arms wrapped tightly around herself.

When they stopped playing, Dawson shuffled back into the kitchen to finish preparing them a meal and Claudia led Sofie into the den.

They sat in comfort in what appeared to be the only room Dawson hadn't renovated. "This room is exactly as I remember it," she told Sofie.

"Look. You see that water mark?" She indicated a ring on an end table. "That's my fault. I put a cup there without a coaster. But Dawson took the fall for me."

"He seems like an exceptional guy. You're lucky you found him."

"He's not my boyfriend."

"Well, whose fault is that?"

"He doesn't think of me in that way. I'm like a little sister to him."

"I wouldn't be so sure about that. I've seen the way he looks at you."

"He hasn't given me any indication that he has interest beyond friendship."

"I'm finding that hard to believe. You're doubtless too busy talking incessantly to notice his advances. Try this. Talk less. Smile more."

"I don't talk that much."

"Sure, you don't." Sofie chuckled.

Claudia remained quiet for about one minute before babbling on again. "Whatever he's cooking smells superb, doesn't it?"

"It does."

She went on and on about nothing until he finally called them to the table.

Morning arrived too soon for Claudia. She held the pillow over her face and groaned. She slowly rose to her feet and shuffled down the hall to wake Sofie. Claudia had slept on the pullout couch in the den. Sofie had used the guest room.

The two of them trudged down to the kitchen and Claudia rummaged through Dawson's refrigerator and cabinets. She put together scrambled eggs and sizzling bacon. The smell of the bacon must've lured Dawson to the kitchen because he filled the doorway with his massive form as he wiped sleep from his eyes. "Smells delicious."

"Sit down. We'll thank the Lord for our bounty and then we can eat."

"Sounds like a plan." Dawson sat at the kitchen table and led them in asking the blessing on the food. "What do you ladies want to do today?"

"Do you need help with the farm chores?" Claudia asked.

"I can always use a hand, but at the way Sofie is crinkling her nose, I think we ought to think of something a little less distasteful to her."

"You could take me home," Sofie said.

"I don't think that's such a great idea. Can't you relax for a while? Maybe watch old movies or go horseback riding?"

"I guess I could watch movies. I always enjoy a good movie marathon."

"Fine, it's settled. You two will settle in for a movie marathon and I will take care of the farm chores."

Claudia hadn't seen much of Dawson on Saturday. He was serious about working on the farm while they watched movies. He joined them for dinner and then ran right back out the door. When it got dark, he glued himself to the computer until it was time for shut-eye. She was starting to wonder if he was avoiding her.

He had found his way to the breakfast table and was gobbling up the last bite of his hash browns.

"We've got to hurry out of here if we are going to make it to Edinsville in time for service," Claudia said between bites.

"We're not going to Edinsville. We're going to my church in Dushore."

"Why would we do that?"

"Because your safety is our utmost concern and I'm not convinced it's safe for you to be in any of your usual haunts. We need to protect you from that animal out there."

"Don't you think you're being a little overprotective?"

"No. I don't."

Sofie pointed her fork at Claudia. "He's right. You shouldn't go to your dad's church today or any of the places that this crazy person might expect to find you. On an entirely separate note, I'm not going to church anywhere. I'll wait here until someone can drive me back to our apartment."

"So, you're going to lecture me about staying safe, but you're going to run back into danger."

"You forget one important fact. He isn't after me. He's after you. The note was written to you. Not me."

Claudia sighed. Dawson scowled, but in the end, they both had to admit she was right. Although, who could say if the mad man would use Sofie to get to Claudia? After church they would drive Sofie back to Williamsport, but she wasn't happy about it.

Dawson watched Claudia as she sang along with the hymns. He enjoyed seeing her get lost in the music. He sang along, but quietly enough that he could still hear her lovely soprano. He sat closer to Claudia than necessary. For some reason, he needed the closeness. He didn't touch her, but there was electricity radiating from her. He couldn't believe he was having these thoughts. Claudia was young. She was barely an adult. She wasn't ready for the type of meaningful relationship he was looking for. He needed a wife not a child to babysit. He knitted his brows together and tried to concentrate on the preacher. The message wasn't a light one this morning, but regardless of the depth of the sermon, Dawson wasn't being drawn in. He heard the preacher discussing the realities of hellfire and reminding the congregation that it was up to each of them to ensure their friends and family heard the gospel message. Dawson thought about Sofie stubbornly refusing to attend church with them this morning. He was sure Claudia had witnessed to Sofie, but her heart was hardened, and she didn't want to hear about the love of Christ. He prayed silently that the Lord would do the preparatory work in her heart to allow her to be more receptive to the message of Christ's love.

The pastor did an altar call and a couple of people walked to the front of the church and knelt down in prayer. The deacons took the time to speak quietly with those folks as the service wrapped up with another song.

Claudia peered up at him with an expression he'd seen on her face many times when she was younger. It was something akin to hero worship. He would have to remind her that he wasn't a hero. He was a red-blooded man. With needs that would be difficult to repress if he were to continue spending so much time with her. His desire to protect her warred with his desire to be rid of the temptation she brought. If he let her walk away from his life, his desire for her would fade in time. He wouldn't completely withdraw himself from her as long as she was in danger, but he hoped that he could at least separate himself emotionally. She would be okay if he spent the day working after they dropped Sofie off. In fact, he'd leave her at the farm while he took Sofie home. That way he wouldn't have the lengthy ride back in the truck alone with her.

He opened the door and she climbed up into his truck. He caught a glimpse of her calves as her flouncy skirt shifted. He decided that distance was what he needed. He pushed his fingernails into the skin of his palms and counted to ten. Distance. Yes, that was it.

He made his suggestion for Claudia to remain behind when they got back to the house. She didn't argue. She hugged Sofie and told her this would all be over soon. Claudia cried as they said goodbye. You would think they were going to be separated forever. He figured they didn't have much confidence in law enforcement finding the man who sent the package. If it was a man.

The ride to Williamsport was quiet. Sofie wasn't much of a talker. She had little to say, but what she said usually demanded attention. He was impressed by her quiet strength. He thought Claudia had chosen her best friend and roommate well. This girl would be a nice contrast to Claudia's extravagance. Where Claudia liked to dress expensively and was always made up and perfectly groomed, Sofie was relaxed and dressed comfortably. She didn't worry about people judging her appearance. Simply running a brush through her hair and throwing on clothes was enough. Extras, like jewelry and makeup were unnecessary. Or at least that was his take on her. He could be totally off-base. He remembered a comment Claudia had once made about Sofie trying to hide herself, so she would blend in. He didn't think of Sofie as beautiful, but she was average looking and certainly likable. She seemed like good friend material.

He dropped her off and hurried back to Dushore. He was uncomfortable with Claudia there by herself. He had a state-of-the-art security system, which might be overkill for the Endless Mountain region of Pennsylvania, but he had highly confidential computer software on his systems that he was responsible to protect. He couldn't let his clients' programs become compromised while he was working on them. Today, he was glad he had that security.

Chapter 8

Claudia watched out the sliding glass door in the kitchen as the black bear and her cubs moved around the yard. It was surprising to see them during daylight hours. She'd always thought bears were nocturnal. She enjoyed watching the cubs climb a tree while the mother raided the bird feeders. She watched with delight as the mama bear set the suet she'd pried out of the feeder onto a rock and hustled her cubs over for the grub. After their meal, the mama bear watched through the glass door at her. The bear meandered across the lawn and up onto the porch while Claudia stood frozen to the spot. The bear wouldn't be able to get into the house, but there was a niggling doubt that told her it might be able to open the door. After checking the lock to make sure the door was secure, her feet finally came unglued from the spot, so she retired to the den. She thought that maybe if she got out of the bear's sight that it might lose interest and go away.

A few minutes passed before Claudia sneaked back into the kitchen to see if the bear family was gone. She didn't see them anymore. Relief flooded through her. It was awesome to see the creatures out in the wild, but she didn't want to invite them in for supper.

He watched through the binoculars. They were powerful. Military grade.

The huge black bear appeared to be pounding on the glass door. Claudia backed out of the room. He kept the binoculars focused in on the family of bears. What would they do next? The action was more than he'd gotten in all the days he'd spent watching. His mission was to watch. Simply watching. He'd recently allowed himself the luxury of doing things outside of the scope of his mission. The letters. They weren't part of the mission. He'd written them anyway. The targets deserved to know their risk.

He watched and waited. Finally, the big man came back. He watched through the window as Claudia pointed excitedly at the spot where the bear had been. She was animated in her movements. She made an easy target of herself. Why didn't she stay away from the windows? He admired the sleek interior of her neighbor's home. The man had style.

Suddenly, he was back in the war. He tried to avoid the incoming barrage of bullets, but he'd been hit. He screamed. His battle buddy pulled him to safety. Pressure was applied to the wound, but he was losing blood. Consciousness was fading fast.

Claudia greeted him at the door with a grin. "You'll never guess what happened while you were out."

"The bad guy found you and you defeated him singlehandedly."

"Not even close."

"Darn."

"There was a black bear family in your yard. The mama bear tried to come in the kitchen door."

"Wonderful." He said with more than a touch of sarcasm. "I guess I won't be able to feed the birds for a few months. Those pesky bears destroy the feeders every spring."

"Don't they usually come by at night?"

"Evenings mostly, but sometimes they sneak in during the daylight hours."

"Did Sofie seem okay when you left her?"

"Yes, she seems to be a relaxed person by nature."

"Most of the time she is, but sometimes she hides her feelings well."

"I guess you can see through her facade?"

"Not always. She can be a master at disguising her emotions."

"Interesting. Are you an expert on her emotions?"

"No, but she's my best friend. I know her."

"I've got a lot of work to do. Why don't you check out the bookshelf in the den? Maybe you can find something worth reading. I'm going to try to catch up on work."

"Okay. Sure." She shuffled off into the den to do as he suggested.

When she reached the den, she read the spines and found mostly non-fiction titles. Few appealed, most of the books were theology and she didn't want to read them. There were also programming manuals that she figured would be over her head. She finally settled on one of the few fiction titles among the books. *The Scarlet Letter*. She'd read it in high school, but remembered it being an interesting study in hypocrisy, judgment and condemnation. It might be able to take her mind off of her real-life drama for a short time. As she settled down on the couch and tried to read the words, she kept getting pulled back to her conversation with Dawson. He seemed to be in a hurry to get her out of the way, so he could work. Did he have a deadline, or was he sick of her being around?

Dawson sat down to dinner. Claudia had once again commandeered the kitchen and found ingredients to make a satisfying meal. She'd thawed ground venison and made a meatloaf that was unlike anything he'd had before. Was that bacon in there? Delicious, but he'd better get her out of his kitchen before he gained weight. "This is marvelous."

"Thanks, it's Mom's recipe. She has the best ones."

"She's quite a woman, your mom is."

"Yes. She is. How's your work going?"

"It's going. It'll keep me busy most of the evening, I'm afraid."

"Oh. That's too bad."

"Don't worry, I'll still be able to get you to school in the morning if you feel safe enough going."

"Yes, I'd like to go to school. I don't want to get too far behind. I'm thinking that I'll stay at my apartment tomorrow night."

"I don't think that's such a good idea."

"Well, then I'll stay with Stella. I don't want to be in your way."

"Who said you were in my way?" Dawson asked.

"It's a feeling I have."

"A silly notion. Don't be ridiculous. You're fine here. I'm enjoying your company."

"I'll decide tomorrow. Right now, I'm going to wash up these dishes."

"No, I'll get them," he said.

"It sounds as if you've got a lot of work to do. You should get back to that."

"I guess so."

The telephone rang, interrupting his plans. Not that he needed to work, his deadline was weeks away, but he needed to keep distance between himself and Claudia for his own sanity. He picked up the handset on the second ring. "Hello."

He listened for several minutes as Jim explained that the police believed they'd found the body to which the heart belonged.

"Do you want to talk to her? Yeah, sure, I can tell her. Don't worry. I'll keep her safe tonight, but she's already saying she wants to go back to her apartment tomorrow."

He listened to Jim argue that Claudia could not return to her apartment until the situation was resolved. "She's not that easy to convince, but I'll try. Any news on your friend?" He got the update on Joe's condition. "I'm glad to hear he's pulling through. Goodnight, Jim."

"So, as I'm sure you figured out, that was your father."

"What did he have to say?"

"His friend, Joe, is doing much better. They are confident that he'll be okay. He'll have serious scarring, but they think he'll make a full recovery."

"That's wonderful news."

"Yes. But in other news, they found another body. This one missing a heart. Your dad thinks you should stay here a little longer."

"So, I'm supposed to put my life on hold indefinitely?" She got up and scrubbed the dishes with more force than necessary.

Dawson walked up behind her and rubbed her shoulders. This was not the distance he was seeking, but he couldn't stay away from her. "It's going to be all right. You'll get through this."

The doorbell rang, interrupting the moment. Claudia rushed to answer it only to be pulled back by Dawson. He bopped her on the nose with his knuckle. "Stay here. You know better than to rush toward what could be an unknown threat."

"Do you think 'an unknown threat' would ring the doorbell?"

"I'm acting with an abundance of caution. I would suggest you do the same."

"Yes, sir." She saluted his back as he hurried to get the door. A moment later he was back with her sister in tow.

"Where are the boys?" Claudia asked.

"Mom has them. I thought we could use some sister time."

"Sounds wonderful. I've been around enough testosterone lately."

"Preaching to the choir, girl."

"I guess so. I don't know how you do it, surrounded by boys all day every day."

"It's a blessing and a curse."

"I'll leave you ladies to it."

"You don't have to go," Stella said.

"I get the impression you want girl time and I'm all male. I have work to do anyway."

After the sound of his footsteps on the hardwood floors faded, Stella sat down at the table and stared at Claudia who was still drying dishes. "So, what's going on with you two?"

"What do you mean?" Claudia almost choked on the piece of gum she'd popped in her mouth after dinner.

"I mean, he's been taking an awfully big interest in keeping you safe lately. Why?"

"How should I know? I guess he's a nice guy."

"We've known Dawson Montgomery our whole lives, of course he's a nice guy. That is not what this is about. Something is going on here and your nosy sister wants to know more."

"Nothing's going on with Dawson and me." Claudia turned around to meet her sister's intense stare. "I'm not saying I would be averse to the idea. But at this present moment, nothing is going on. I'm getting mixed signals."

"What kind of mixed signals?"

"One minute, I think he's interested in me. A hand lingering on my shoulder. A long look. A special smile. The next minute, he's all business and acts like he can't wait to get away from me."

"He's being a man."

"How can you say that? Jason was never anything but attentive and was never indecisive."

"Jason is not a typical man."

"And Dawson is?"

"No. He's something special. You know I was always crazy about him. He's almost family."

"Almost doesn't count."

"No, of course not. He's the type of guy that I would love to see you fall in love with."

"I'm not sure I want to get involved with anyone. You know what I went through with Sameer."

"You know Dawson is not Sameer and you wouldn't have to worry about that sort of thing with him."

"My head knows that. My heart says not to trust him."

"Okay. I get that. What's Dawson got around here to snack on?"

"Real food or dessert?"

"Dessert of course."

"I think I saw apples, and there's vanilla ice cream in the freezer. Apple crisp sound acceptable?"

"Delicious. I'll peel the apples while you mix the other stuff." Stella rose to find the apple peeler.

"Should we share with Dawson?"

"Of course. We wouldn't be good guests otherwise."

As they got busy preparing dessert, Stella brought up recent events.

"How are you holding up?"

"I guess you have the latest updates?" Claudia asked.

"Dad called before I put on the news, so I was spared the report, but I got the gist of it from him. You didn't answer my question though. How are you holding up?"

"I'm not sure. I'm somewhat frightened, but at the same time, I feel safe here. I don't enjoy having my life put on hold because of some wackadoodle mad man, but I don't mind being here, out in the country away from the everyday madness of life. Honestly, I've never been more confused."

"Are you going back to school tomorrow?"

"I don't know. I don't want to miss too much school. I want to finish my classes, so I can start my life."

"You don't have to finish your classes to begin your life. Life started when you were born, believe it or not."

"You know what I mean."

"I do. You mean, so you can begin your career. Don't let a career define you. There is so much more to life than what one does for a living. I was going to be a wildlife biologist, that didn't happen, but I'm happy with my life. I love being a mother and a wife. I wouldn't trade it for any career path. I know you're majoring in art, but what do you plan to do with it anyway?"

"I had been considering continuing my education, so I can teach art, but I don't know. I'm nearly finished, and that would mean another year, at least."

"I can't see you as a teacher. You don't have the temperament for that."

"Wow. Thanks."

"Would you prefer I lie to you? You're an artist. You need to create. Whether its paintings or music, it's who you are. Teaching would stifle that. It's too regimented."

"You might be right. I guess that's why I didn't plan for it. But as I get close to graduating, I'm wondering what use this degree is going to have for me. How am I going to support myself?"

"I'm not sure you should try to answer that question tonight. Don't try to write someone else's story. Be yourself and live your life. Even a well-planned life, will veer from its charted course. Stick the apple crisp in the oven, will ya? Let's try to enjoy what's left of my free time. We'll talk about something more fun. Let's talk about Dawson. I think you could fit a dime in his dimples."

Claudia put the food in the oven and set the timer. "You, dear sister, are strange. His dimples are great though. I always loved a guy with dimples." Claudia thought about Sameer. He had dimples too. She should miss him more, but she didn't. She missed the idea of him, the relationship she'd thought they had, but she didn't miss the actual man.

Chapter 9

Dawson settled in at his desk. He'd driven Claudia back to school and his mind was on her. He hoped she wouldn't put herself in any risky situations. The computer cursor blinked at him, reminding him that he was supposed to be working. Computer programs did not write themselves. He was working on a classified project for a major pharmaceutical company.

The refrigerator beckoned. Maybe he'd think better after a glass of sweet tea. Pouring the tea, he walked back to the desk and reviewed the work he'd done over the past few days. The deadline was far enough away that he wasn't pressured, but the program he was attempting to develop was complicated. He didn't want to procrastinate until the last possible minute. His mind needed to be clear to make sure he wasn't missing anything. Therein lay the problem. His mind was anything but clear. He couldn't focus with Claudia constantly invading his thoughts. Maybe prayer would help.

Scooping up his Bible from the end table, he meandered into the den. He tried to read the words, but they blurred together on the page. The Lord's words were eluding him. He silently prayed, but didn't feel close to God. He wondered if God was upset with him for something, but he had no idea what he'd done wrong. Deciding to take his horse out, he headed toward the stables. His gorgeous paint stallion waited for him as he lay the blanket and saddle on Huckleberry. It was a chilly day, but he hoped the cool air would help clear his cluttered mind. They set out at a brisk pace, but it wasn't long before he had Huckleberry galloping across the fields. They flew past the grazing cattle and walked down across the creek. The mountainous terrain on this side of the creek rose sharply, but they slowed down and climbed the steep trail. The peace and solitude they would find at the end of the trail couldn't be beat. He hopped off the horse when they reached the campsite. They wouldn't be staying the night tonight, but he'd spent many nights sitting at this fire ring dreaming of the perfect future. Could it be within his reach now? He'd figured out the career. He had it made as a freelancer. He earned more than enough to cover his expenses and save for the future. There was no shortage of funds for charitable giving, so he was content with his career and finances. The farm offered him an outlet for his restless energy. All that was left for him to find was the woman he was meant to share it with. He wanted a family, but he wasn't willing to settle for the wrong girl.

The women he'd met all had an agenda. A few had wanted him to buy them stuff. Some wanted to be coddled and taken care of. Most didn't share his passion for God's word. He'd learned many women who claimed to be Christian were Christian in name only. They didn't have the desire to truly know God. Christianity to them was a set of rules. It involved going to church on Sunday and following a list of dos and don'ts. Getting to know the living God didn't fit into their superficial religion. They were cultural Christians.

He wanted to be with a woman who loved Christ more than she loved him. He couldn't live up to the expectations that most of the women he'd dated placed on him.

Only Christ could fill the void in their lives. When he was younger, he'd tried to fill that void with women and booze, but it had been a failed experiment. He'd learned God was the only one who could fill the empty place in his heart. He was content with things as they were, he had a sturdy foundation on the solid rock of his faith.

It was only recently he'd yearned for something more. Spending time with Claudia had rekindled the desire for love. It had been a distant dream until he'd come back in contact with the girl who had been like a sister. He didn't think of her as the girl next door. In his mind, that was Stella. Claudia was the girl next door's bratty little sister who never left him alone for a minute. She followed him around, messing up his plans. When he snuck into the woods for a cigarette, she'd show up with her pigtails and dirty face and he'd have to walk her home instead of lighting up.

His friends even found her annoying. She wasn't always around. They showed up for weeks during the summer and occasional weekends. Remembering brought a smile to his face. Suddenly being around her wasn't such a hardship. Was she in the same place as him spiritually? She was a pastor's daughter, so, of course, she knew the Bible, but did she truly know the Lord? He thought so, but he had to be sure. He'd seen her behavior do a one-hundred-eighty-degree turn. Remembering the thought of the tight leather skirts he'd see her wearing years earlier brought warmth to his neck and cheeks. Thankfully, she'd toned it down immensely. He hadn't seen her smoke a cigarette or curse up a stream in recent times, but, if truth were told, he hadn't seen her much in the past few years. She'd matured, but did her maturity extend to her faith? Would Jim approve of him taking out his daughter? He had to find out the answers to these questions before he proceeded.

Claudia walked across campus toward her next class. If English Lit had been any indication, it was going to be one of those days when she'd wished she'd stayed in bed. Kicking at a tiny stone that lay in the path, she jumped when her cell phone rang. Pulling it out of her purse, she held it to her ear. "What's up?"

"Do you need me to come out there and pick you up after school?"

"I promised Sofie we could hang out tonight. Raincheck?"

"Are you sure it's safe for you two to be hanging around there?" he asked.

"What am I supposed to do? Hide out in the country for the rest of my life?"

"No. Only for a couple more weeks. Until the police get this wacko."

"I can't live my life in fear. How about we hang out on Friday? I'd love to come up and stay at my Pop's for the weekend. I'll meet you up there."

"Sounds great."

"Pizza at Pop's. Friday night? How's seven?" she asked.

"You're on."

Claudia's mood improved. No longer did she desire to kick things. She wanted to get through her classes, so that Friday would arrive. Her sudden mood swings had her perplexed. *What has gotten into me lately?* Picking up her pace she hurried along to her sociology class. She couldn't for the life of her figure out why she'd decided to take that course.

Claudia took her seat in the second row. "Hi, Professor Borneo."

"It's Doctor Borneo, my dear."

"Sorry." She opened her binder to retrieve her homework.

The lecture droned on. Doctor Borneo was a nice guy, but he was a boring lecturer. He did most of his teaching with PowerPoint slides and didn't engage the class with personal stories and interesting tidbits. His classes involved him reading highlights from the text book on a projector. Not at all stimulating.

Her thoughts drifted back to Dawson again while she was supposed to be watching the screen. Why was he stuck in her mind so many of her waking hours?

After sitting through what was possibly the most boring class of her life, she hurried back to her apartment. There was an envelope stuffed in between the storm door and the entrance door. She tore open the letter and sat down to read it.

You don't know me. And I'm sorry to have to tell you this, but you know the killer. I warned Steven about what was going on with Judy, but he didn't save her in time. I'm warning you to get away from here before the killer gets you too, but, one can assume, you won't listen. Be careful. I'll be watching.

She was still sitting there with the letter in her trembling hand when Sofie showed up a few minutes later.

"What's going on?"

"Read this."

Sofie took the mysterious letter from Claudia's trembling hands and read it. "Call the police. And then call Dawson."

"Do you think it's from the killer?"

"I don't know. Perhaps. But if he's watching you, you need to get out of here."

"That's the thing. Someone has been watching me at the farmhouse too. They sent me a video. A month ago."

"Does Dawson know about that?"

"No. I didn't think it was important at the time."

"You still packing?"

She chuckled at the way Sofie asked the question. "Yep."

The smell of fresh tar assaulted the senses of the Marine sniper. His elbows dug into the roof as he focused his attention through his scope and forced his other senses to quiet. He watched Claudia walk to class. He'd been keeping tabs on her for months. When she entered the building, he left the roof. Her class would be over at 1400 hours.

He made his way back to his perch well before class was dismissed. He watched as she made her way to her little bug. He'd stay on the sidelines, unless she needed him, but someone had to keep watch. Provide cover. Sooner or later, he'd fill her in on the mission, but for now, he'd simply watch and wait. That was what he'd been trained to do. Watch and wait, perfectly still until it was time for the kill. He let his breath out slowly, it would be so easy.

Dawson wasn't sure if he was supposed to pick up the pizza or if Claudia was bringing it. He didn't want to bother her at school, so he bought a couple of pizzas that he could stick in the oven. He figured that way they could have pizza whether Claudia brought it with her or not. He smiled at the thought of seeing her again. He knew he shouldn't let her get to him. She was another girl who would surely find something better to do in a few weeks. Why was he letting himself fall for her? What was the point? Did it have any chance of working?

Her beautiful face flooded his mind. He knew she was too pretty for him. He didn't put much stock in outward beauty. He was perfectly content to date an average-looking woman if she was something special inside. He'd dated a few women, but they'd disappointed him.

Claudia was different. She enjoyed music, so they could share that. She rode horses, so they could do that together. She loved this land, so they had that. But most importantly, she shared his faith. So, what was he afraid of? She could be the woman he'd been waiting for. If only he'd opened his eyes sooner, he might've noticed her. The doubts flooded in again. Maybe they should end it before it started.

The thoughts wouldn't leave him alone. He built a fire in the hearth and relaxed on the couch, allowing the room to heat up before Claudia's arrival. The smell of the wood burning was comforting. He'd much prefer she join him at his place, but he understood that it would be improper. It was okay for a weekend, when she'd been in danger, but he couldn't continue to have her there indefinitely. She needed her space and privacy. He'd have to watch out for her safety from a respectable distance. If he had her under his roof too often, he might not be able to control his physical response to her presence. He had more respect for her than to test himself.

After a short wait, she pulled into the driveway. He was happy that he would be celebrating his birthday with the raven-haired beauty. She might not know it, but he'd enjoy spending his thirty-third birthday with her. He smiled when she walked in the door.

"It sure is cozy in here."

"I thought you'd appreciate a fire."

"You thought right. I brought pizza. I'm sure it's cold, but we can stick it in the oven for a while to warm it up."

"It smells delicious. I'll stick it in the oven while you get your jacket off and settle in."

"Works for me." She handed him the pizzas.

"How much do you think we can eat, just the two of us?" He headed toward the kitchen.

She raised her voice to be heard. "We'll undoubtedly devour one of them, but Stella and Jason might come by later with the kids. I brought enough for them, too." He squashed the disappointment that they wouldn't be alone, reminding himself that supervision was a positive thing.

"It's clearly enough for everyone, but I brought a couple of frozen pizzas, so if they show up, we'll be all set."

"Thanks. You're always thinking," she said. She settled down on the love seat and curled both feet up under her and a throw wrapped around her legs.

"Comfortable?"

"Yes."

"I'm glad." He sat beside her and leaned in toward her. He grabbed a bag from the floor in front of her and handed it to her. "I have several movies in here, pick your passion. We'll put it on as soon as the pizza warms up."

"Maybe we can just talk for a while," she said.

Oh, no. Nothing favorable ever comes from talking. "Okay. Sure."

"I've been wondering what's going on with us. So, I thought I'd ask. What is this?"

"Just two old friends hanging out on a Friday night."

"That's all this is. Just two friends spending Friday night together?"

"Why? Did you think it was something more?" He wanted to kick himself for saying something so stupid. Why would he intentionally say something he knew would hurt her? He wanted this to mean something, why couldn't he admit that?

"My mistake. I guess I was reading more into your kindness. Forget I said anything. Wait. Do you smell gas?" She stalked off into the kitchen and he followed behind her and watched her slam the oven door when she realized that the oven was still cold. He'd forgotten to light the pilot. Where was his brain? It was an old gas oven.

"I'm going to open the back door. I forgot to light the pilot, so we've got to air out the house. Would you go out to the living room and open a few windows."

"It's kind of cold for that, but sure."

After waiting a few minutes to make sure all the gas had dispersed, Dawson lit the pilot light and set the temperature on the oven again. "Sorry about that. I have a more modern oven at my place and all I have to do is turn the dial."

"You were obviously trying to blow us to smithereens. It's a good thing neither of us is a smoker."

"I remember a time when you would steal cigarettes from me."

"That was a long time ago," she said.

"Doesn't seem that long ago."

"Is that the problem? I'm like a little sister and you can't stop seeing a child when you look at me?"

"Sometimes, yes. Other times, not at all. I see you as a fully-grown woman most of the time. You're a beautiful woman. The problem is that I don't want us to get into a relationship and have you change your mind. I'm not moving. Your family will most likely keep the place next to mine. I value your friendship and the friendship of your parents. We have so much to lose by taking a risk."

"Sure. That's true." Her head dropped down as she tried to hide the tears he could see forming in her eyes. "I shouldn't let myself care, but I thought there was something between us worth exploring."

Dawson wiped the tears away with his thumb. And pulled her to him. He gave up the internal struggle and bent down to kiss Claudia. Her lips parted without hesitation as she received his gentle kiss. "We'd better go watch the movie and eat our pizza before we get into trouble here."

He made no move to end the embrace.

At the sound of the front door opening, Claudia jumped back and slammed her head into a wall cabinet. Dawson stepped back to allow her room to escape his embrace. When she had turned back to the oven, he walked into the living room to greet her family.

He was as casual as could be when he greeted her sister and brother-in-law. "Stella. Jason. Great to see you. Need help getting the kids out of the car?"

"That would be great," Jason said as he put one of the car seats down on the living room floor. Dawson followed Jason from the house. Claudia entered the room and greeted her sister. "You look exhausted. Have you been getting any sleep?"

"Not much. The babies have been running me ragged. I'm spent. I've been looking forward to coming out here and having help with the kids. Jason's always working, and I'm left with everything else. Somehow, when I get here everything seems better. Calmer. It smells great in here by the way. Nothing quite like a fire."

"Fresh air will do that to you. You live in the country though, so not sure how this is getting away."

"I think it has to do with it being our childhood retreat. And not only that, but getting away from the responsibilities of my house. I don't have to worry about this house being spotless. I can sit down and relax with my family."

"Makes sense."

"So, why were you blushing when I walked in the room? Something going on with you and Dawson?"

"No. Yes. Oh, I don't know. He kissed me."

"Seriously? Now that's interesting. Dawson Montgomery is a careful man. If he kissed you, he must be seriously into you."

"I think it was a mistake. He pretty much told me it would be a mistake for us to get involved before he kissed me."

"Yet, nevertheless, he kissed you."

"Yes."

"The plot thickens."

Dawson walked back into the room with a sleeping child. "Where do you want him?"

"Would you carry him up to the blue bedroom? If it's not too much trouble?"

Once Dawson had climbed the stairs, Stella spoke again. "Give him a chance. He'll come around. He's just scared."

"Maybe," Claudia said.

"What are you hens squawking about?" Jason asked. It was clear from the grin on his face that he'd heard more than enough to deduce what was happening.

Warmth radiated from the fire blazing in the fireplace. Claudia sat on the floor and leaned back against the overstuffed chair Dawson was seated in. The kids were sleeping soundly, and Jason and Stella were on the love seat. The couch sat empty across the room. The movie was forgotten on the end table.

"How did you handle it when Stella went missing? Didn't you lose your mind?" Dawson directed his question to Jason.

"Yes, I went crazy. Just ask Mac. I can't believe he let them hire me after all the trouble I gave him with that investigation, interfering at every turn. The whole thing was a nightmare."

"I'm glad I didn't know about it until it was over. I would've been there trying to help."

"I believe it. I see how protective you are of Claudia, and from what I understand, you and Stella were close."

"That was ages ago. Both girls are much younger than me, so we didn't spend much time together. Stella and I did talk from time to time."

"It was way more often than 'from time to time' as I recall," Claudia said.

"It only seemed that way. Your family wasn't here often. So, it was only a couple of nights a year for a couple of years that we spent any time together."

"I guess that's true," Claudia leaned back and rested her eyes.

"When Stella's stalker kidnapped her, I think we all lost it. Especially, when that second girl went missing and the news made it sound as if it could be a serial killer. It was terrifying," Claudia glanced at her sister.

"Isn't that what we're dealing with now?" Stella ran her fingers through her hair, trying to untangle her curls.

"On that note, what do you think will happen to this place with your grandfather gone?" Dawson asked.

"Dad's not interested in living out here. And the upkeep is too much for him to keep it on unless it gets regular use. He'll probably have to sell. Unless, Claudia wanted to move here after she graduated," Stella raised an eyebrow and glanced at Claudia.

"I don't know about that," Claudia said.

"Why not? It would be perfect. You could get away from our parents and have your own space. Nobody breathing down your neck. You could easily spend most of your time painting. And, someone would be here to take care of the property. If it was something you couldn't handle on your own, you could call someone to come out, but at least you'd be here to know if the heater went or something happened with the plumbing. Whatever."

"I don't think Mom and Dad would agree to that plan."

"Of course, they would. It makes perfect sense."

"Maybe we can talk to them about it, but until they say it would work for them, it doesn't matter what I think of the idea."

"I'd like to hear what you think of the idea," Dawson rubbed Claudia's shoulders.

"Why?"

"I'm interested to know your thoughts. To see how that mind of yours works."

She inspected the ceiling and contemplated what she would say. "I love it out here. I'd have plenty of inspiration for my work simply looking out the windows. It would be a lot of responsibility and upkeep, but I'm sure Mom and Dad wouldn't kill me on the rent, so it would be cheaper than living in the city. I guess I'd be interested in living here. At least for a while."

"No other reason why you might want to live out here?" Dawson asked.

"I guess there is. I mean, I could bring Ava out here, too." She gazed up at him with a twinkle in her eye. She knew he was fishing to see what she thought about being near him, but she wasn't about to bite the hook.

"You're right. Ava would be great company. She couldn't be alone all the time though. You would need another horse. If you brought Stella's horse, then your mother's horse would be alone, right?"

"Stella and Jason keep their horses at their place. But Dad has a horse now, so Mom's wouldn't be alone. I guess I'd have to get another one to keep Ava company."

"Who'd ride it? You could keep Ava at my place."

"Why is it even a discussion? I haven't talked to Mom and Dad, and I don't think for a minute they'd go for this idea."

Jason spoke up. "I think you're wrong. I believe Jim will think it's a splendid idea. He doesn't want to sell the place, so this is the perfect solution. Do you want me to ask him for you? You seem nervous about the idea."

"I'm not sure. I'll let you know."

"It's getting late. I think I'd better head home. Thanks for the hospitality." Dawson got up and she followed him to the door, watching as he drove off.

She closed the door and leaned her back up against the solid wood. "I don't know if I can be so close to him. He's going to break my heart if I let him."

Jason smiled. "I think that you're making a big leap there."

"He said he wasn't interested. Does he have to tattoo it on my forehead for me to get the picture?"

"I don't care what he said," Jason said. "That man is interested."

"I agree with Jason," Stella grinned.

"You always do."

"Not always," Jason said.

Chapter 10

C laudia pulled the big Kitchen-Aid mixer from the cabinet and dumped in ingredients. She was going to make pumpkin muffins before Stella got up and then she'd make the rest of the breakfast of scrambled eggs and hash browns. She wished she had a mixer like this in her apartment. She thought about Sofie alone back at school and how sad she'd been the last few days. She couldn't figure out what Sofie had going on, but she knew it was more than the trouble surrounding her. If only she would speak up.

She got down on the floor with matches to light the pilot light. As she lit it, the front door opened, and she heard Dawson's voice. "Anyone up?"

Getting up too quickly, she smacked her head on the top of oven as she tried to extricate herself from it. She growled, "Yes, I'm up."

"I can see that. And ever graceful." He watched her as she poured the batter into muffin tins. "Any reason the door was unlocked? I brought the key, but didn't need to use it."

"Jason must've unlocked it when he went for his run. Can I help you with something? Or are you early for breakfast?"

"I've been thinking. Let's be crazy and try this. Okay?"

"Try what?" she asked, knowing full well what he meant but wanting to make him squirm.

"Try us."

"What changed between yesterday and today?"

"I'm not sure. I guess I'm not willing to miss out on the chance at something great because I was too afraid to try."

"What about how I feel?"

"How do you feel?"

"I'm not sure. I'm scared."

He pulled her into his arms and hugged her close. "I'm scared, too." He held her for several minutes, but she broke the embrace when she heard tiny feet running down the stairs. "We're about to have company."

"I can hear that," he said.

She returned to cooking and he came up behind her and rubbed her shoulders. A newfound hope stirred within her. Maybe this could work.

The hyacinths had bloomed through the snow a couple of weeks earlier. This morning, Claudia had seen the first daffodil bloom. The appearance of the bright yellow flower, left her feeling hopeful. Something about spring brought out the best in people and nature. She loved watching the birds on their migration, returning from their winter haunts.

She drank her coffee and thought back to her recent past. How could things be so out of whack? Her anxious, uptight nature was shifting and she wasn't sure why. She remembered how hysterical she'd been when Stella had been kidnapped. She'd had an altercation with Jason over cracking her chewing gum. She'd had so much tension built up in her that she'd felt like that piece of gum herself, as if at any moment she would crack and there would be nothing left but a gooey mess. Something about her had changed. She no longer panicked when everything fell apart. A level head usually prevailed.

Dumping the dregs of her coffee into the flower pot on the counter, Claudia turned her attention to more important matters. How was she going to make up for missing Dawson's birthday? When her father called, he'd informed her that Dawson had turned thirty-three the day before.

What could she do for his special day? He'd been by earlier, but begged off claiming he had to work. She could see how he used the work excuse whenever he was worried that he was getting too close to her. She rifled through the cabinets to see if she had everything necessary for making a cake. She did. Except for candles. She could pick some up. She turned on the mixer as Stella entered the kitchen.

Stella plopped down in a kitchen chair and waited for the mixer to go quiet. "What are you making now?"

"A cake."

"Haven't we had enough junk for one day?"

"We missed Dawson's birthday yesterday."

"He didn't mention it."

"Of course, he didn't. Dad did. So, I thought we should at least make him a cake. I'm sure he'll be back over for dinner."

"I think you can bet on that."

"What's that supposed to mean?" Claudia tapped Stella with a wooden spoon.

"You figure it out."

"Are you guys staying for dinner?"

"We'll be here until after dinner tomorrow, unless you want to get rid of us sooner."

"Why would I want to do that?"

"Oh, I can think of a few reasons." Stella grinned.

Claudia shook her head and stirred the cake mix. "I talked to Dad about moving out here after I graduate."

"What did he say?"

"He thought it was a capital idea. He has to talk to Mom first, of course, but at least I have an in with Dad."

"Awesome. I think you'll love being out here on your own. It's the perfect place. Quiet. Solitude."

"You sound jealous."

"No. I love it here. It's part of my roots, but our place is perfect. I wouldn't trade it. I like the idea of having you here. That way I can come by and visit you any time I want and leave my mess for you to clean up when I go home."

"Spoken like the sister I know and love."

Dawson's fingers banged away at his keyboard. Why couldn't he get this girl out of his head? There was more to life than women. Yet, even while preparing a lesson for the youth group he led on Sunday nights, she crept into his mind.

Life could so quickly complicate itself. Only a few weeks ago, he'd been breezing through life without a care in the world. One call from Jim to check on the house and suddenly he'd gone from single and happy to lonely and desperate.

Glancing at his watch, he forced himself to refocus. He needed to find references in the Bible, so he could present a clear message to the youth.

Once a rough outline was drafted, he prepared to go out. It would be so easy to go back over to see Claudia. Ridiculous that he couldn't stay away for one day, but, nevertheless, he would go.

Inspecting his image in the mirror, he contemplated whether he should shave. He'd been allowing the stubble to grow for a few days. If only he could hide his emotions as easily as the stubble hid his face. Deciding not to shave, he grabbed a jacket from the hook beside the door and hurried up the path to the stables. He saddled up Huckleberry and headed out for a ride. He'd end up next door soon enough. For now, he rode his paint off the beaten path hoping to clear his head.

It wasn't long before they were crossing the creek and heading into the mountains. Huckleberry suddenly reared up and Dawson hung on tightly. Looking around to see what spooked the horse, he saw a fox making a meal of something with a lot of feathers, presumably a chicken. He stroked the horse's neck and whispered to him until he calmed.

They veered off on a trail he rarely rode. It led to an old cabin. It was a structure from the 1800s. It was impressive how it held up over the years. The door hung loose from the frame and the space between the logs allowed the wind to enter in, but the sturdy stone fireplace remained intact. There was a loft that hung down on one side, but otherwise the building was strong. He'd thought about restoring it and allowing visitors to come through, but the thought of people on his land left him unsettled.

Hopping off his stallion, he noticed something wasn't right. Someone had been there. And recently. He wasn't sure how he knew, but he was sure of it. Then he noticed the prints. Not the usual bear prints, or deer prints that surrounded the cabin, but boot prints.

Entering the cabin, he found a sleeping bag and lantern inside. Heading back to the house to get a game camera, he considered what possible reasons the intruder had for being on his land. Was this simply a squatter or something more sinister?

Dawson was greeted by Stella's smiling face as she opened the door. "Where have you been all day, stranger? Five more minutes and you would've missed dinner."

"Sorry about that. Found out there's a squatter on my land and had to set up a camera to catch him."

"Seriously. I didn't think people squatted on land out this way. Thought that was more of an issue down south."

"I guess I got too comfortable. The security on the main part of the property is excellent, but the other side of the creek doesn't have any."

Stella closed the door. "Claudia was putting dinner on the table when I came to answer the door."

"Smells spicy. What is it?"

"Chili and corn bread for the adults. Hot dogs for the kids, so I guess you're getting a hot dog."

"Hilarious."

He followed her into the dining room and watched as Claudia set bowls of steaming chili on the table. He could get used to seeing her as a picture of domesticity. Claudia glanced up, smiling when they made eye contact. "I thought you were standing us up."

"Would I do that?"

"Yes. I believe you would."

He settled down in an empty chair where Claudia had placed food for him. The smell of spicy chili and warm corn bread caused his stomach to grumble. He was looking forward to this evening with the McIntyre family. He missed meals like this with his own family.

Jason entered with a tray of corn bread. "So, Dawson, what are your intentions with my sister-in-law?"

Dawson watched as Claudia choked on her water. When she regained her composure, she swatted Jason hard in the back of the head.

"Well, I, uh—" Dawson started.

"I was kidding, but it is fun to watch you stutter and see Claudia flip out."

The chili was cooked the way he liked it. Enough spice to make it flavorful and give it a kick, but not so much that you couldn't eat it without shoveling bread in every other bite.

When they finished dinner, he was surprised when Claudia turned the lights out and brought out a cake covered in candles.

"How did you know?" he asked after they sang happy birthday.

"Dad mentioned it. I wish he'd have told me before I came up yesterday, then I could've been prepared."

"This was sweet of you. What flavor of cake is under all that frosting?"

"I guess you'll have to cut the first slice and find out." She handed him the knife.

He cut into it and put slices on the paper plates she'd set out. It was a rich chocolate cake with chocolate mousse layers and ganache. She'd made it before and he was crazy about it. Too rich to eat regularly, but a nice special occasion treat.

"Do you have ice cream, Aunt Cwaudia?" Glen asked.

"I think there's some in the freezer." Claudia stood to check.

Dawson followed her into the kitchen, his plate in his hand. "You didn't have to go to all this trouble. It takes you hours to make that cake. I remember when you made it for your grandfather's birthday."

"I wanted to make it for you." She was standing at the counter scooping out a couple of bowls of ice cream for the kids.

"Thank you." He moved behind her and kissed the back of her neck gently.

"I have news," Claudia said.

"You do?"

"Dad said he thinks my moving out here is a welcome idea. He still has to talk to mom about it, but it sounds like I might actually move here." He wondered how well he would be able to control himself with her next door. All the time. He turned her around and gave her a light kiss on the lips. Then stepped back. If he stayed in here, they would both regret it and the kids might not get their ice cream before it melted. He took a deep breath and slowly walked back to the dining room.

Chapter 11

Claudia tried to make the brush glide across the canvas, creating the image in her mind, but her inner turmoil was reflected on the page. The mountains were ominous. Her emotions were raw and open. She thought that anyone looking at her could see through to her soul. Her thoughts turned to Sofie. It had been a trying week for both of them, but Claudia had her family and her Lord to see her through.

She glanced up at the clock and realized she'd only been in class for twenty minutes. Time was dragging today. She sensed the professor coming up behind her. She felt his hand on her shoulder as he leaned forward to look at her work. "Brilliant, Claudia."

"You don't think it's a little dark?"

"Brilliantly dark, darling."

Brilliantly dark? What is wrong with people?

"I'm not happy with it. I'd like to start over."

"No, no, no! This is fabulous work. Keep at it. I can see this work being chosen for the show next month. That is if you don't mind attending it after graduation? Don't give up on it. Life isn't all sunshine and roses, dear. Sometimes life is dark, and you've captured the essence of foreboding. Keep at it."

I supposed he is right. He walked away, and she added touches of green to the valley in the scene. He was right. It was fine. It simply wasn't her style. She didn't like it. She spent the rest of class alternating between perfecting her work and staring at the clock. Had she only been here for an hour? Time was dragging.

When the clock finally struck one, she hurried from the room as if she was running from a monster in her nightmare. Which was about right, since that was exactly what she was doing. Only this nightmare was real. She rushed up the stairs to her apartment and ran smack dab into Sofie at the top of the stairs. "Sorry. Didn't mean to run into you."

Sofie's eyes were damp. "Don't worry about it. I'm headed to class. I'll catch you later." She picked apart a crumpled tissue.

"What happened? You okay?"

"I'm fine. It's nothing."

"Are you sure? Maybe I can help."

Sofie let out a bitter laugh. "Not likely. Look it's nothing, okay? I'll be around tonight. Maybe we can catch a movie. That is, if you won't be too busy with Dawson."

"Sure. Okay."

Claudia watched Sofie lumber down the stairs. Something was definitely wrong.

Claudia rolled over in bed and put the pillow over her head. She'd been dreaming and wasn't ready to get up and face reality.

In her dream they were royalty. She and Dawson walked along a rocky shore, waves lapping at their ankles. They had two boys following along behind them, collecting seashells. The boys were about a year apart in age. They had their father's melted chocolate eyes. They wore attire indicative of sixteenth-century Scotland. He was wearing a long kilt as were the boys. She was wearing the tartan as well, a skirt that would reach her ankles, if she hadn't been holding it up. She had her head covered with a plaid scarf. Up ahead was a cave and they were walking toward it. A fine mist lay over the shore and there was a chill in the air. The breeze that caressed her face smelled of salt and fish. She was content. They were together, and they were headed toward their castle. As they reached the cave, she saw it on the bluff. They needed to enter the cave to get into the castle, but before entering, she woke up. The dream was a vivid one, but it wasn't real. She wasn't royalty and there was no castle.

Reality set in. It was time to rise from the warmth of her bed and walk down the stairs. She could turn the key in her car and head back to town. She never should've left Sofie last night. Yet, she couldn't bear to go back there. If she'd been a better friend, she would've gotten her to talk when they watched the movie last night. Something was obviously wrong. Instead, she'd allowed her to dodge questions and left well enough alone. Clearly, Sofie wasn't ready to talk about what happened and she wasn't in any mood to force the conversation.

She finally rolled over and sat up on the edge of the bed. *Okay, I can do this.* The room was cold, the embers of the fire had cooled during the night. It took a moment to get her bearings. She'd slept in the main house the night before, not wanting to walk out to the loft.

She loved the old house. She'd enjoyed the comfort of the fire and the thousand-thread-count cotton sheets on the king-sized bed. Her usual comfort at being in her own space above the garage was replaced with a deep sense of belonging. This was where her family had put down roots and she was here for the long haul. Less than a month until graduation. Claudia was ready. If only the killer would be caught. She wanted to enjoy her sense of accomplishment, but the threat of danger constantly hung over her. A giant guillotine ready to be released.

Her thoughts were disturbing to say the least. She needed to let off steam. She ran next door to get dressed. Throwing on a pair of jeans, she grabbed her 380 and a box of ammo. It was time to shoot off a few rounds. After that, she'd face reality.

She stapled the target to the big wooden board where her family had been shooting for decades. Beyond the board was a steep mountainside hill that ensured any stray bullets would end up in the ground instead of flying off into the unknown. She hit mark every time, making a tight circle on the heart of the silhouette. She filled the chamber with practice rounds again and emptied the magazine into the target one more time, this time aiming for the head. When she completed shooting, she reloaded her pistol with hollow points, chambered one, flipped the safety on and slipped it back into the holster at her waist.

Claudia had been trained to protect herself. After her sister had been kidnapped, her father had insisted that they both take self-defense courses, and then he'd taught them to shoot. She'd enjoyed the lessons more than Stella. Claudia had taken to it like a goat to a hill. She'd liked it so much she'd enlisted with the Marine Reserves.

The sound of a quad broke into her thoughts, followed closely by Dawson's voice shouting over the sound of the engine. "What on earth are you doing? Trying to give me a heart attack?" He turned the machine off and stared at her with a look of incredulity.

"What? Don't you want me to be able to defend myself?"

"Maybe a phone call to let me know you're going to be shooting, so I don't think you're in the midst of a shootout would be nice."

"I hadn't considered that you would think a thing. Gun shots are a regular occurrence out here, and nobody thinks anything of it."

"I grew up here. I know everyone shoots, but someone has been threatening your life, and you just about cost me mine with this stunt. I flew over here so fast, I rolled the quad."

Ignoring her frustration and anger at being yelled at like a child, she rushed to his side and ran her hand along the wound on his face. How hadn't she noticed the blood streaming down his cheek when he'd pulled up? "Come on in the house and let's get you cleaned up."

"I'm still ticked at you, young lady."

"Young lady? Seriously? Get over yourself, old man. I'm going to get something to clean out that wound. You could make my life easier by joining me in the kitchen."

He followed closely on her heels. Using his arms to heft his weight up, he sat on the counter. "If you think I can reach you up there, you're daft." He hopped down and sat in the chair she pulled out for him. She filled a container with warm, soapy water and a rag and dabbed at his wound. "I think you need stitches."

"I'm not getting them."

She couldn't stop the grin from forming.

"What are you smiling about?" he asked.

"I was just thinking about the dream I had last night."

"Were you dreaming about me, princess?"

She laughed out loud as she thought about how well his comment fit with the dream. "I'm no princess."

"Maybe you should be. Tell me about the dream."

"I think I'll keep it to myself."

He reached out and tugged on her braid. "A woman full of secrets."

Claudia perspired despite the cool morning air. She slowed her steps from a fast jog to a brisk walk to allow for a period of cool down. As her heart beat slowed, she moved closer to the river's edge. She loved these brisk mornings out near the water. The fog hung low and left the river looking surreal. She walked toward the water's edge to the log where she usually rested before returning to the parking lot.

As she approached the log, something seemed out of place. Upon closer inspection, she spotted an arm draped over it. She was about to speak to alert the person that she was there when she realized that her words would go unheard. There was no life left in the woman. Her body had been dumped. The killer must've left it here knowing she frequented this trail. Someone was making every effort to terrorize her. Her heart raced, and she looked around to see if someone was watching. There was nobody around, but she felt a presence. The birds were quiet. None of the usual sounds of nature.

She didn't scream. The parking lot seemed farther away then usual. She began the trek back to it. If she could make it back to her car, she might be able to get a cell signal. She picked up her pace, jogging back to the lot.

After grabbing a towel from the passenger seat, she wiped the sweat from her brow before dialing 911. They asked her to wait at the location until the police arrived. She knew she'd be there much longer than that. They'd want to question her, again. She should've eaten breakfast before her jog. This was going to be another long morning.

The shrill ringing of the telephone interrupted Dawson's work. He took a last look at the computer screen before reaching out to answer the handset.

"Stella? Wait. Slow down."

"Claudia found another body," Stella said.

"How? Where?"

"Jogging by the river."

"She knows she's in danger. What's she doing out jogging by herself?"

"I don't know. She's mule-headed."

"Yes, she is. Where is she now?" Dawson asked.

"She left the police station a few minutes ago. She's headed out to the farmhouse. Would you check in on her?"

"Of course. I won't let her out of my sight."

He disconnected the call and stared at the computer screen. No sense in trying to finish his work. He wouldn't be able to concentrate. He'd go out and clean stalls for a while giving her time to drive to the farmhouse. Physical labor would release some of the anger building up inside him.

He'd like to string that mad man up by his toenails somewhere. Not a Christian thought, but enough was enough. Claudia didn't deserve this sort of torture. When he'd given her enough time to make the drive, he headed next door.

As soon as she was able to make her trembling hands turn the key in the lock and push her way into the house, Claudia sunk to the floor in the foyer and prayed.

I'm scared. I know I'm supposed to trust that you're with me, but this is terrifying. Why this poor girl on the trail? I don't think I've ever seen her before. Is it a coincidence? Or is he trying to scare me?

Please keep Sofie safe. Please protect her. Draw her near to you.

Mostly, please stop me from shaking. I can't stop the shaking. I need your help. Let this guy get caught. I don't want to see anyone else die. You and only you understand the why behind this, if there is a why. Can any good be found in something so horrid? I don't think so, but I guess free will didn't come with limitations, huh? Help me!

Please make me see your will more clearly. I'm falling apart down here.

Claudia was startled by a noise. Looking up she realized Dawson was standing in the doorway watching her pray. For a moment she wavered over how she felt about him watching her pray, was it an intrusion into her privacy or simply a new level of intimacy? She decided it was the latter and she was ready for it. Maybe his presence was an answer to prayer. She smiled up at the man who had come to mean so much in such a brief time.

Was he the real deal? Was she too young to think about forever? He reached down and took her hand in his, pulling her from the floor and into his arms. He held her close. She snuggled her face in close to his chest and breathed in his unique scent, a mixture of hay, soap, and something spicy.

"Why is this happening?" she asked.

"I don't know, but none of this is your fault."

"How do you know that?"

"I just do."

"Did you get any photos on your trail cam?"

"I haven't checked it yet."

"Stella called you?"

"She thought you might appreciate the company. The real question is why didn't *you* call?"

"I don't know. I suppose I should've."

"Yes, you *should* have."

Claudia sighed and let the tears flow. "I'm glad you're here. I need you here."

Dawson held her in his arms for several minutes. She stood on her tiptoes and kissed him.

He made a growling noise and deepened the kiss. A few minutes later, he pulled himself back and held her at arm's length. "Squirrel, I don't know how we keep ending up in situations where I have so little self-control, but I think we should move into the other room and put a little distance between us."

As soon as he broke the contact, she felt hollow. Like a part of her was gone.

Claudia watched as Dawson pulled out a notebook from her grandfather's desk and made notes. He wrote down the names of the victims, the locations where they'd been found, and their connection to her. Seeing it on paper was frightening. It brought the whole thing into focus.

She had a connection to all three victims. She only knew Judy personally, but one of the others was connected to her because of the heart package. And she'd found the other one. There was no denying this all came back to her.

"There are a few things I haven't mentioned. Don't get mad. I didn't think they were important at first."

"What kinds of things?" Dawson had a sharp edge to his voice.

A shiver shot up Claudia's spine. "Someone sent me a YouTube video that first morning when I ran into you here."

He growled low in his throat. "Do you still have it?"

"I do. I had to figure out how to download it. They don't make it easy. The link in the email doesn't work anymore, so whoever put the video up took it back down."

"You didn't think it was important enough to tell me about this?"

"I didn't want you to think I was a silly girl who couldn't take care of myself."

"Keeping it from me made you seem more like a silly girl than telling me would've."

The words hurt, but he wasn't wrong.

He raked his fingers through his hair. "Are you a computer expert? Do you know how to trace digital footprints? How, exactly, were you going to take care of this yourself?"

"I told the police about it when they questioned me about Judy's murder."

"Have you heard from them about it since?"

"No."

"Not surprising. I'll follow up on it. Is there anything else you're keeping from me?" His tone was biting.

"No. You know about the tire being damaged and plugged. I don't know if that's related, but it seems it could've been an attempt to get me to have to pull over somewhere where I might be vulnerable."

"I'd forgotten about that. That might well be the case," Dawson said. "If the shop still has it, I'll take the tire to Jason, maybe he can have the state police lab look into it."

Claudia shrugged and leaned back on the couch, wishing she could fade into the cushions. She'd managed to anger him. Again.

"I'll grab my laptop and show you the video," Claudia said.

"Fine. I can dig around and see if I can trace where it came from."

"I deleted the email."

"Not a problem. I should be able to get to it anyhow."

She ran outside and up the stairs to the loft apartment. Life was getting complicated. Now that her adult life was about to begin, everything was going zonkers.

She wasn't gone for more than five minutes before returning with the laptop.

Opening it, she located the video download and played it for him.

"You seriously didn't think this was important enough to show me? He was here? Recording you?"

"At the time, I thought it could be Sameer playing a sick joke."

"Even after I told you about the squatter on my property? What if it's the same guy?"

"I didn't think of that. The cabin is on the other side of your land, it isn't even close to here."

"It's next door. Whether it is five miles or fifty yards. It's the place next to yours. Easy access to spy on you."

"Great. I should sleep well tonight."

She went to the kitchen. When she got back, Dawson was staring straight ahead. She placed a mug of steaming cocoa down in front of him. "What is it?"

"I think I've got it."

"Got what?" Claudia took the notebook he held out to her.

"They're all Christians."

"So? More than seventy percent of Americans claim to be Christian. Hardly relevant."

"No. There's more to it than that. All the victims were last seen at Independent Baptist churches on Wednesday nights. He's killing people after they leave church."

"Judy was at church on a weeknight?"

"That's what it says here. She'd gone to that church's prayer meeting for the first time the night she was killed. Looks like her roommate gave them her last-known whereabouts and they confirmed her attendance with the church members."

"Where are you getting all this information? Did the police give it to you?"

"Don't worry about that. Suffice it to say that I was able to dig it up from the investigation files, and it looks to me as if Christians are being targeted. I'm surprised they haven't released that. It could save lives if people were on guard leaving services."

"Why would anyone target Christians?"

"I don't have an answer." Dawson stood and stretched.

"Are you going home?"

"No. I'll stay on the couch. You should stay upstairs tonight. No sense in me being here if you are going back to the loft."

"There are plenty of bedrooms. You don't have to sleep on the couch."

"It's fine. I'll be more alert if I stay down here."

"I want you to stay, but I don't want to be that big of an inconvenience. I've already messed up your day enough."

"I'm staying. Grab some of your stuff from the loft and move it over here. You're talking about moving in after graduation. You might as well start the transition tonight. Do you need some help?"

"Let's worry about that over the weekend. For now, I want to get some sleep. I'll just grab my nightgown."

Chapter 12

Claudia opened the door to her apartment as Sofie hung up her cell. Tears spilled from beneath the thick frames of Sofie's glasses.

"I thought he liked me. I must be a fool."

"You are not a fool. Who is 'he' anyhow? Is this what you were upset about before I left?"

"A guy I've been seeing. A professor. He claims he's feeling guilty about dating a student."

"Did you remind him you're about to graduate?"

"It was an excuse to dump me. I'm not a complete fool."

"I knew you were seeing someone, and he'd obviously upset you last week, but it was clear you didn't want to share the details."

"I didn't want you harping on me about how it's unethical for a professor to date his students. Or how immoral it is for me to spend nights at his place."

"I wouldn't have done that."

"You would've. Ever since Stella's kidnapping when you 'found religion' you're an entirely different person. You're constantly lecturing me."

"Am not."

"Are too. He didn't belong with me at any rate. He could have any girl he wanted. He should be dating a girl that looks like you, not me."

"Why must you put yourself down?"

"You're the one who's always suggesting I change my wardrobe, cut my hair, or put on makeup."

"That doesn't mean I don't think you're pretty. It means I think you could be even prettier if you let yourself."

"Well, apparently I'm not pretty enough for Johan. I'm going to get ready for class. If I have to face him, I'm at least going to look my best."

"Now that's the right attitude."

Claudia tried to figure out which professor had the first name Johan. Maybe she could look it up on the university website. She was sure Sofie wasn't ready to spill it. Most likely, she didn't even realize she'd let the name slip.

Staring at the mirror in the staff bathroom, he took inventory of his ragged appearance. He could use a haircut. It would wait until he returned. He read the dates on the airplane ticket. This wouldn't do. He had stuff to do in Pennsylvania. He couldn't be rushing off at the whim of his boss. There were more important things to accomplish here than what could be done at a useless conference in Tampa. Settling down in his office chair, he considered how he might use this trip to his advantage. If he was out of town, it would provide an alibi, but how could he arrange to be in two places at once? It was a lengthy drive. A plan came to mind, and the corners of his mouth turned up in a slow smile.

This could work. This could definitely work. He typed up an itinerary, printed it, and stuffed it into his briefcase. Walking out of his office he whistled a tune. He couldn't recall where he'd heard the song, but it flowed effortlessly. He threw the briefcase in the back seat and made himself comfortable in the driver's seat. It was time to prepare for his trip.

The drive home was uneventful. He breezed in the door and rushed upstairs. After packing his carry-on bag, he grabbed the roll of plastic and lined the trunk once more. He'd have to stop soon, or else, move again. Probably, the latter. He'd need to move soon. Couldn't be too careful.

He fingered the cross he kept in his pocket. A trophy. He loved the feel of the smooth gold in his hands. So many deceived by a false message of love. He knew better. The game had begun a long time before he was born. He was only playing his part. Sooner or later they'd find out the truth. Sooner or later the deception would end. The car would be parked in long-term parking. He'd make sure to get a ticket stub to prove it.

He'd paid the homeless man in crisp hundred-dollar bills. He watched as the man, who was about his size and build—with the same color hair—walked into the conference. He would drive a rental car back to Pennsylvania while his alibi attended the conference. *Brilliant.*

If he drove all day, he'd make it back in time to leave another body where it would be found, get a good night's sleep, and make it back to Florida to catch his flight out. His alibi would be rock solid. The homeless man had agreed to meet up with him to pass on the conference materials before he caught his flight back to Pennsylvania. The man was the only real flaw in the plan, people talked, but he could take care of him too if necessary. No reason to get queasy worrying about it, he was a tool. A means to an end. He'd make sure to kill him in a completely different manner and set it up to look like a drug deal gone wrong.

The drive took forever. The traffic brutal. Too many records with a flight, so he'd decided to drive. He was much less likely to be noticed in a car. Millions of people traveled Interstate 95 every day. He was getting tired of moronic imbeciles cutting him off though. He ought to switch lanes to avoid the on-ramps, but driving in the left could bring unnecessary attention. If he received a traffic violation there would be a record of this trip and that would not do. It wouldn't do at all.

He arrived at their apartment Wednesday evening. He watched for a couple of hours. There was a light shining brightly in the tiny living room. Getting out of his car, he slowly made his way to the window. It was slightly higher than eye level for him, but, if he stood on the railroad tie bordering the garden, he could see inside.

Claudia wasn't in there.

Considering his options, he walked back to his car.

"Professor, what are you doing here? I thought you were going to that conference in Florida?" His eyes met those of one of his favorite students. Too bad she'd made herself his next victim.

"Oh, Shelly, life got in the way as it tends to do. I've been thinking about your project. Do you have a few minutes to discuss it? We could drive down to the coffee shop and talk."

"Um. Yeah, I guess. I was heading to prayer meeting, but I can spare a few minutes. I'm usually the first one there in any event."

He held the passenger door open and she scooted inside. What exceptional luck. She was one of them. Not a number five, but close enough.

As he drove away from the city, she spoke. "We're going the wrong way to get to the coffee shop."

"We're not going to the coffee shop, dear." She reached for her door handle, but he had the child locks engaged. "I'm sorry, dear. You're a beloved student. Unfortunately, you caught me where I wasn't supposed to be. Class won't be the same without you."

He drove calmly toward his home in the woods. She started clawing at him and he had to pull over to restrain her. He reached out and hit her hard in the temple. Then he bound her wrists with the zip ties he kept in the console.

She hadn't regained consciousness when they arrived. He had to drag her out to the patio. He attached her to the chain and ambled inside to wait for her to wake up.

When she woke up, he was watching her. Yes, she was definitely praying.

Thoughts of his wife and children filled his mind. He could use a shot of whiskey to numb the pain, but he'd given up that vice the night they died. If he hadn't been drinking away his troubles, they'd still be alive. He'd have been home, smelled the smoke, and saved them.

His wife had been a praying woman, had prayed every night for him and their four children, but God hadn't answered her prayers. If there was a loving God out there, He wouldn't have allowed them to die that fatal night. He stood and paced the floor for several minutes.

He didn't want to kill her. She was such a lively student, but sometimes sacrifices had to be made. Something akin to regret washed over him as he went outside to end her suffering.

The tinny sound of the doorbell called to Claudia. She hurried to answer it.

"What's the matter, Sofie?"

"I found another body." She locked eyes with Claudia. "It's Shelly. I didn't want to tell you over the phone."

"Where? How?"

Sofie paced in the foyer. "The killer left her at our place. Not just the heart this time. Her whole body. Badly mutilated. I lost my breakfast."

"What on earth does this psycho want? None of this makes any sense? I guess he left her for me?"

"He wrote your name in blood on her forehead. I was with her late yesterday afternoon, we'd been studying in the library. She said she had to leave in order to make it to prayer meeting in time. About an hour later, I came home and watched a movie. I was chilling on the couch gorging myself on popcorn while some psycho was brutally murdering my friend. I was so mean to her, Claud. Horrible. All because she was ditching study group to go to church on a weeknight."

Claudia grabbed Sofie by the arm, and led her toward the den. "This is not your fault. No matter what you said to her. You didn't cause this."

"I was with the police for hours. They're going to question you again, too."

Dawson walked up the stairs and let himself into Claudia and Sofie's apartment. The girls had gone to the station, so Claudia could answer some questions. Again.

He stood at the front window looking out at the police activity. All these hours later, and they hadn't finished up their investigation.

A tall man walked up the steps to the apartment. He was familiar. It was that professor Claudia had been cozying up to when he'd picked her up back in March.

"Hi. I think we've met before. Claudia's boyfriend, correct?"

Dawson nodded.

"I'm Professor Marcus. Is Sofie around?"

Dawson was surprised it was Sofie the man was here to see. "No. She and Claudia are down at the station."

"Oh. Okay. Thanks."

The man started back down the stairs, but a uniformed officer stopped him. Dawson eavesdropped.

"Hello, sir. Noticed you over at the residence there. Can you tell me what you were doing?"

"Yes. I was there to see Sofie. I saw the police cars and ambulance there earlier."

"Are you friends with her?"

"Yes. We're close."

"Do you have a few minutes to answer questions?"

"I guess. What sort of questions?"

"Would it be too much trouble to ask you to come to the station?"

"I'll come down if you think it will help."

Dawson watched as the man got into the back of the police car. When they drove away, he walked into the kitchen to make coffee. This was going to be another long night.

Claudia sat beside Sofie in the interrogation room. She'd answered their questions. There wasn't anything different she could tell them.

An officer told them they could go, so they started out. On their way down the hall, they passed Professor Marcus coming in with another officer.

"Professor Marcus, what are you doing here?" Claudia asked.

"I'm trying to help the police."

"We're heading back to our apartment. See you in class tomorrow."

"I'll see you both tomorrow. Have a pleasant night."

"That was weird. What do you think they want to ask him about?" Claudia asked.

Sofie stared at the ground as she walked, not meeting Claudia's eyes. "I have no idea."

"It's not as if he's a forensics expert or anything. He's an artist. Maybe that's it. They might want him to do a sketch of the killer. Do you think someone saw him?"

"Again. I have no clue. I don't have an in with the cops."

"Well, it's got me wondering. Did I tell you, Jason had that tire looked at by the state police lab?

"Did they find anything?"

"No fingerprints, but they found DNA. A strand of hair was stuck in the fix-a-flat. It matches the DNA they found under one of the victim's nails. They don't have anything to compare it to, yet."

"Well, at least it's something."

"They need a break in the case."

Chapter 13

hat black-haired-vixen Claudia was getting under his skin. Her friend had found the body. That ought to keep the cops guessing. They might even think it was Sofie he was after all along. He growled low in his voice as he thought about her sitting there in his classroom with her Bible open. Did she think it somehow made her a superior person to read a compilation of books written by forty different men? Didn't she realize those words were written by people, not by the Holy God she claimed wrote them. What a fool. They were all fools.

If she hadn't opened that book in his class and wore that cross around her neck, he might've continued to find his victims at churches, but she got under his skin. He was going to add her to the list of victims, but he must proceed with caution. Changing his modus operandi could throw suspicion on him. It wasn't to his liking that so many of the victims had a connection to the school. Heart girl didn't. Her name was Jolene. It was in her wallet. He'd picked her up at the same church where he'd happened upon Judy. He usually liked to canvas churches, but he'd been on a tight deadline, so he didn't have time to scope out an unfamiliar one. He'd wanted to frighten Claudia. It had worked perfectly. She'd missed a couple of days of classes before she'd gotten brave and returned. He fingered the newest cross in his pocket.

He'd left the body for Claudia, but he knew it would frighten Sofie, too. Sofie wasn't his intended target. She wasn't religious. Didn't even attend church as far as he could tell. He'd watched her as she vomited from the top step into the garden below. Exactly where he'd been standing the night before. He saw her pull out her smart phone and assumed she was calling the police. He'd loved writing Claudia's name in blood on the victim. It excited him to see Sofie find the present he'd arranged so carefully. Luckily, nobody had been by to see the body before Sofie found it. Too bad Claudia had missed it.

It was before dawn when Dawson removed his bandage as he stared in the bathroom mirror. There was going to be a scar. He should've gotten stitches after he'd rolled the quad.

It was going to be another long day. He couldn't concentrate on his computer work, so he'd spent yesterday plowing fields, preparing them for hay. They sold some of the hay they harvested, but most of it was kept for their own animals. He gave some to Jim for the McIntyres' horses. Their families had worked together to ensure that both had enough of everything. The McIntyres had provided his family with beef and mutton before they'd started raising their own. They would share venison with each other, as needed. The dynamic had changed since Jim's father passed away. And Dawson's parents weren't around either, but Dawson would share whatever abundance the Lord blessed him with.

He wondered what Claudia was doing. He surely couldn't sit back worrying about her all day. He needed to get out there on the tractor and set his mind on the business of farming.

He didn't stop until the heat of the day when he trudged into the house to get a lemonade and a sandwich. Looking at the caller ID, he saw that Claudia had called about two hours ago. He berated himself for not having checked sooner as he dialed her number. Directly to voicemail. He couldn't sit here waiting for her to call, but he didn't want to miss her if she tried again. What to do? He stuck the cordless phone in his back pocket and headed back out. If he stayed close to the house it would work. He worked close to the house before taking off to feed animals. As he walked toward the hay barn the telephone rang. "Hey."

"Hi, Dawson. Sorry to bother you. It's been crazy down here. I don't know where Sofie is."

"What do you mean you don't know where she is? Do the police know?"

"I mean exactly what I said. I called the police, and they didn't take me seriously. With everything that's been going on, you would think they would, right? I hope something didn't happen to her."

"Do you need me to come out there? Help you search for her?"

"It probably won't be productive to search, but I'm going to try anyway. I wouldn't mind your company."

"You've got it, squirrel. I need thirty minutes to feed animals and get changed. I'll be there in about an hour and a half. Would you do me a favor and go to the coffee shop or something until I get there? I don't like you being in that apartment by yourself."

"It is kind of creepy. I'll meet you at the coffee shop down the street from my place. I warn you though, I'm going to want to sleep in my own bed. At my apartment. In case she comes home."

He thought of her black hair sprawled on his pillow. He sucked in a breath. "I'll sleep on your couch tonight. That way I'm here to protect you. If we don't find Sofie tonight, we'll figure out what to do tomorrow."

"I'll see you shortly."

He disconnected the call and fed the animals, giving them extra since he wasn't sure what time he'd make it back in the morning.

Claudia sat at the table in the coffee shop and stared out the window. She had her laptop open in front of her and was looking at her final paper for her history class. It wasn't her best work. Exhaustion overwhelmed her, and she leaned her head back against the chair. "May I join you?"

It was Sameer.

"I'm waiting on someone."

"Well, it appears he stood you up."

"What makes you think it's a 'he'?"

He settled into the chair across from her. "You've been in here by yourself for nearly an hour. I walked by earlier. I didn't expect you to still be here when I got back, but I'm glad you are. Can we talk? You've been ignoring me. I know I screwed up, but I think it's time for you to forgive me. We'll move on."

"I'm not moving on with you. It's over."

He continued as if she hadn't said a word. "We can get married and then the sex issue will be solved. You won't be having premarital sex and I won't have to continue to wait."

"How romantic. You want to marry me, so we can have sex. Thanks, but no thanks."

"What's going on here? Who are you?" Dawson towered over the table, his body blocking any exit that Sameer could take.

"We're just talking. I don't think we've met." Sameer put on a charming smile and held his hand out to the larger man.

Dawson ignored it. "I think it's time for you to skedaddle." He moved aside, so Sameer could get past him.

Once the jingling of the door stopped after Sameer's exit, Claudia laughed. "Thanks for your help, George."

Dawson settled into the recently vacated chair. "George?"

"Of the Jungle. You were awfully cavemanish, don't you think?"

"Not at all. I heard what he said to you. What a creep. You're not marrying that scum of the earth."

"Oh. I'm not? You get to decide my future now?"

"This shouldn't even be a discussion. What a loser. What hole did he crawl out of?"

"You're right. This shouldn't be a discussion. What Sameer and I do is my business, not yours."

"You're not seriously considering his offer, are you?"

She wasn't, but she wasn't going to give him the satisfaction of knowing she'd been disgusted by Sameer too. "Sameer and I dated for a couple of years. He is the only serious boyfriend I've had, and he mostly treated me well, until recently."

"What happened recently? Why is the charming Sameer no longer in the picture?"

"Don't worry about that."

Dawson sighed. "So, moving on from your loser ex-boyfriend, what are we going to do about finding Sofie?"

"Where have you been? Claudia has been worried sick." Dawson switched on the light and watched as Sofie tried to shield her eyes from the brightness.

"Dawson?"

"Who else would be here? Sameer?"

"Wait. What? Where is Claudia?"

"She's in bed. I sent her up a couple of hours ago. She waited up most of the night for you. After we searched the campus and surrounding areas."

Sofie rubbed her eyes. "I've been out. I fell asleep."

Dawson raised an eyebrow.

"What's it to you anyhow?" She yawned.

"After everything that you two have been through in the past two months, you're asking me that?"

"I guess I should have left a note when I went out. I didn't think it was a big deal." She hurried past him into the tiny kitchen. "Want coffee? What was that nonsense about Sameer?"

"Yes, I'll take coffee."

"And Sameer?"

"The loser showed up last night. He wants to marry Claudia. But I'd still like to know where you were."

"I was out with a man. Is that so hard to believe?"

"All night? Strike that. I don't want details."

"Tell me more about this proposal."

"What proposal?"

"Sameer."

Claudia stretched her arms over her head and yawned as she joined them in the kitchen. "It wasn't a proposal. It was just a conversation. I can handle Sameer without either of your help. Where were you? I was sick with worry."

"Look, I'm sorry I worried you, but you do it to me all the time. You head out of here and don't come home. I'm supposed to know you must've gone to your parents' house, your sister's house, or your grandfather's house, and lately Dawson's house. I worry too. Sometimes you call, but not always. Occasionally, I need to get away, too."

"You're always welcome to join me when I go home."

"I'm not asking for an invitation. I don't want to tag along with you."

"You still didn't tell me where you were."

"I was with a guy I've been seeing." ·

Claudia frowned, her brow crinkling. "You think that's smart?"

"I think I'm going to live my own life."

Claudia put her hands up in mock surrender. "Okay, do your thing, but remember that I care about you and I'm here if you need me."

"I know that, but I don't want any part of your religion or your God."

"I didn't even bring up God."

"Not yet, but you would've if I hadn't stopped you."

"No denying that," Dawson said. "You might be surprised how awesome our God is, if you only gave Him a chance."

"You're going there after what I just said." She poured coffee into three cups.

"You'll come around." Dawson lifted his cup to his lips.

"I've got to get ready. I have an early class."

"You don't have a class this early."

"No. It's not this early, but I need to get away from you two, so I'm going upstairs to get ready."

"Okay then."

Dawson could hear Sofie running up the steps. He wished she'd stayed. At the moment, he didn't want to deal with Claudia and she would've provided a buffer.

"Why were you telling Sofie about Sameer?"

"I don't know. I thought you and I had something going on between us, but then I drive all the way here and find you at a table with another man, actually talking about getting married for sex."

"I wasn't talking to him about it! He was talking to me about it. And he wasn't there for long. He got there a moment before you."

"Yeah right! And he began the conversation with 'Will you marry me, so we can have sex?'"

"Those were not his words. You're paraphrasing. And yes, that is pretty much how the conversation went."

"I'm sure."

"You don't believe me?"

"Why would I? I tried to straighten this out last night, but you wanted me to stay out of it, remember? It's none of my business."

He downed the last of his coffee. "I'm out of here. Your friend is home, so you don't need me. I'm going home to the cattle. They're trustworthy. They won't be cozying up to a strange farmer before I get home." He stomped away slamming the front door behind him.

Claudia ran upstairs and threw herself across Sofie's bed. "He's gone." She sobbed, her heart breaking.

"What happened? You guys were fine two minutes ago, getting all 'Jesus loves you' on me. What on earth happened between then and now?"

Claudia couldn't control her sobs and they turned to hiccups. When she finally calmed down enough she shared with Sofie. "I messed up. I told him it wasn't any of his business what happens between me and Sameer. I didn't like him saying such rotten things about him. I still care about Sameer. What he said last night was awful, but how do you throw away a person you thought you loved, you thought you were going to marry?"

"I don't think he's asking you to throw him away. He's asking you to stop seeing him. Enormous difference."

"I don't plan on seeing him, but what gives Dawson the right to say who I see, or don't see."

"You have to decide if he has that right or not, but that decision could cost you any chance you have with him. He doesn't seem to be the type of guy who will settle for coming in second."

"I didn't say he was second."

"But that's what he heard. You might want to go after him. If I were you, I wouldn't let him stew on this too long."

"You're right. I need to go after him. What do I say?"

"I think you can figure that out on your own."

Chapter 14

"Professor Marcus?" Claudia stopped at his desk.

"Yes? What can I do for you?"

"I brought in my project, but I can't stay. I've got some urgent business out of town. Is that okay?"

"I suppose if you must run off again, dear, there isn't much I can do about it. You don't want to get behind with graduation in two weeks."

"I won't. Thanks"

Claudia hurried out to her car and slid in. She adjusted the radio to a Christian station. She couldn't take country music today. Music that would speak to her soul was what she needed. She sang along to the southern gospel hymns, almost forgetting her worries. Almost, but not quite.

When she pulled up outside of Dawson's house, she noticed his truck was parked outside the stables instead of near the house. She trudged over to the stables hoping to catch up with him there, but he was gone. He'd taken Huckleberry out. She threw a blanket over Snowflake and saddled up, hoping she could find him in the back country. There were many trails that meandered through the area. He could be anywhere. She would take her chances and at least try to find him.

She hoisted herself up onto Snowflake's back and headed off in the direction she thought he'd gone. There were fresh horse tracks in the mud, so following them was the best shot she had at finding Dawson. After about ten minutes, she came to a fork in the trail. It was difficult to decide which path to take, but she saw horse manure off to the left, so she went that way. Hopefully, she was right on his tail.

She arrived at the old cabin, but didn't see anyone around. She spotted the sleeping bag and accessories that Dawson had mentioned. She patted the horse on the neck and put her head down to nuzzle her. "Where did he go, Snowflake?" The palomino stared off into the distance with her wide, dark eyes, ears perked up. Rustling sounds got Claudia's attention and the horse took off at a gallop. The jostling threw her off balance, but she straightened herself and held on tightly. When the horse finally came to a stop, Claudia scolded her. "That could've been Dawson and we ran from him when we're supposed to be looking for him." But deep within, she knew it wasn't Dawson. Snowflake would've sensed his presence, and not run off. She turned the horse onto a familiar trail. She would head back to the stables and maybe he would be back soon.

She dismounted Snowflake and put up the tack. While she waited for Dawson, she brushed down the horse. She'd always enjoyed the task. It calmed both her and the horse. Her mind was busy trying to figure out who had been back in the woods by the cabin.

Dawson finally showed up at the stable and dismounted Huckleberry. "What are you doing here? I thought you had class."

"I skipped. We need to talk."

"I'm not sure I want to talk to you right now. You wasted a trip."

"Give me a chance to explain."

"You had your chance to explain last night. And again this morning. You didn't bother."

"I'm sorry. Can we please talk?"

"Go ahead. Talk."

"Can't we sit down somewhere?"

"If you want to do that, then you'll have to wait until I take care of Huckleberry. He had the ride of his life and I'm sure he would appreciate fresh water and a brushing down."

"I'll brush him, while you get his water and put away his saddle."

"Fine." He stalked away.

Claudia sat down at the kitchen table and waited until Dawson joined her before she spoke. "I'm sorry."

"What are you sorry for? My being a fool? My driving out to Williamsport to help you and finding you in the company of your ex-boyfriend?"

"You're not a fool. I should've told you what I thought of his comments, but I was too embarrassed." Claudia twirled a strand of hair. There had to be a way to fix this.

"What were you embarrassed about, that you actually considered his proposal?"

"You know it wasn't a serious proposal." She had to keep her emotions in check if she had any hope of reasoning with him.

"No. I don't know that." His voice got louder. "I only know what I heard, and he sounded serious to me." The legs of his chair scraped against the floor as he pushed it back and stood.

"It was a ploy to try to get me to go back to him. He didn't mean anything he said."

"I think you're wrong on that account. I think he meant every word. He could have the best of both worlds if you took him up on his offer."

"What do you mean by that?"

"I mean, he'd have a beautiful wife, but could still go around town being with any woman he wanted. He would figure if you let him get away with it once, you'd let him get away with it again."

"What makes you think I would let him get away with cheating on me?"

"It's no secret that he cheated on you. If you took him back, you'd be opening the door for him to do it again."

"We weren't married. It's not like he was committed to me."

"You think it would've been any different if you were married? You're a bigger fool than I was when I trusted you with my heart."

"What do you mean you trusted me with your heart? You've never told me you love me or anything of the kind."

"You know how I feel about you. I didn't exactly keep it a secret. Traipsing back and forth to Williamsport. Checking in on you every day to make sure you're okay. What did you think, that I do that for every girl I come across?" He turned his back on her and stalked over to the patio door. He remained silent.

"We aren't making any headway here. You're getting angrier with me. I'm saying I have strong feelings for you. That I don't want to be with Sameer. I want to be with you." Tears filled her eyes as she peered up at him expectantly.

"You should've considered that last night when you told me to stay out of your business. I've got work to do. You can show yourself out."

Dawson bunched his fists up in balls. He'd turned away from her and stared out the patio door listening for the sound of her leaving. Once she was gone, he stalked to the front of the house and stared after her. She sat in her car. Her head down on the steering wheel. He wanted to go after her, but he wouldn't open himself up to the pain she could cause him.

He climbed the stairs and fell backward onto his bed. His scream was muffled by the pillow he pulled over his head. The sound of her car pulling out of the driveway got his attention. She sure took her time leaving. He sat up and stared out the window at the dust cloud she left in her wake. If he were to guess, she wasn't going back to school yet. She'd be next door if he decided he wanted to talk. That would be a mistake. He needed to allow a clean break. If they were ever to be friends again, he needed to let her go.

Why had he let himself get entangled with Claudia? She was like a peacock, pretty to look at, but hard to keep on the farm. They always flew away. Beneath her beauty there was an intelligent and fascinating woman, but he couldn't take the chance on her. Let another man fall for her. Someone who didn't mind risking everything.

He thought about praying and leaving the outcome to the Almighty, but he didn't want to give up control. Although he knew he was holding on to unforgiveness, he wasn't ready to let it go.

Going out to the stables, he grabbed a pitchfork and wheelbarrow and shoveled manure for all he was worth. A profitable outlet for his pent-up energy. He would get that girl out of his system.

Claudia was stunned. She'd expected that Dawson would accept her apology and they would live happily ever after. Okay, maybe they wouldn't have the perfect fairytale ending, but they'd at least be content. And together. Sadly, he had other plans. He was pushing her away, and she didn't know how to fix it. She called her dad.

"Hi, Dad."

"What are you doing at the farmhouse? Don't you have school?"

"Yes, Dad, but Dawson and I had a huge fight this morning and I had to come out and try to make things better."

"Got in a fight over the telephone? Been there. Did you get it worked out?"

"He wasn't on the phone. He'd spent the night. No, not with me before you go lecturing. He slept on the couch. Sofie didn't come home last night, and he came to help me find her."

"Did you find her?"

"Yes, but that's not what's important now. Dawson thinks I still have something going on with Sameer."

"Why would he think that?"

"Sameer was sitting with me at the coffee shop last night when Dawson got there."

"Why were you sitting with him? Especially if you were waiting for Dawson?"

"I don't know. I messed up and Dawson doesn't want to hear about it."

"You said he still stayed the night. Why? If all this happened last night."

"I don't know. I guess he wanted to make sure I was safe."

"Well, that's something. You need to go and fix this."

"I tried already. What more can I do? I said I was sorry."

"Try again. He's stubborn, but he's not stupid. If he sees you're sincere, he'll come around. He's smitten with you. Call me and let me know how it works out." Her father hung up before she could make any more excuses.

After a few minutes of prayer, Claudia took her father's advice. She decided to walk. It was a ten-minute walk through the woods or a twenty-minute walk if she walked down her driveway and up his. But he wouldn't be able to avoid her if he didn't see her coming. She decided to cut through the trail in the woods.

As she set out on the trail over to Dawson's she admired the orioles singing in the tops of the trees. She had a lot on her mind, but the tiny birds calmed her. She was further enthralled when she noticed a catbird eating the blackberries from the wild bushes along the trail. They provided a pleasant distraction from her task. In another month, the gnats would be thick and frustrating, but it wasn't bad now.

She considered turning off the trail and wandering down to the creek to sit along the water's edge and take time to herself. She wiped her hands along her jeans to dry her palms. No. She needed to face this. She'd gotten herself into this mess, she had to confront the situation head on.

She tried to think of a Bible verse that would help calm her, but nothing came to mind. She decided that she was going to make reading her Bible a priority. She needed to find solace at moments like these, and only God's word would provide it. Her dad had tried, but he wasn't comforting. He saw everything as a problem to be solved. If he couldn't fix it, he'd prefer not to know about it, or at least that was how she perceived him. Her mom could be encouraging, but sometimes the hurt was too deep for human support to adequately fill the need.

She was getting closer to Dawson's house, so she slowed her movements, not wanting to face the confrontation to come. As she came out from under the cover of the woods, she watched as Dawson tossed his rifle into the cab of his pick-up truck.

He caught a movement out of the corner of his eye and grabbed his rifle from the truck. The action reminded him that Claudia was still in danger. He was pushing her away when he needed to protect her. When he was able to get another glimpse of movement, he realized it was her. He tossed the rifle back into the truck and walked toward her.

"You're back. You don't give up, do you?"

"You wouldn't accept my apology, but I'm not sure I tried as hard as I could've."

"What are you talking about?"

She walked up to him and placed her lips near his ear. "I'm sorry. Forgive me. Please." The words were barely a whisper.

She was too close. He didn't have the self-control necessary for this test. He growled deep in his throat and kissed her, roughly. He couldn't lose control now. He had to be better than that savage she'd dated before him. He'd wait.

She was worth it. What was he saying? He'd decided that he needed to make a clean break and now he was considering a life with her. Again. Was he coming unhinged? He gazed into her eyes and lost all semblance of self-control. He deepened the kiss. His passion overtook him, and he grabbed her and pushed her against the truck. A moment later reason broke through and he remembered where he was and what he was doing. "I've got to walk away, squirrel. Don't follow me. I need a few minutes."

"Okay." Her lips were formed into a pout. She wasn't going to protect herself from him. So that meant he had to be the level-headed one. He walked inside and splashed cold water on his face and neck. After a few minutes he rejoined her.

"We need to go somewhere public. How about the diner? You up for pancakes?"

"I'm starving." He could hear the slight quiver in her voice. She swiped at the wetness on her cheek.

He held the truck door open for her and she climbed up, moving his rifle to the back seat as she slid in. As soon as he closed his door, he realized that the space inside the truck wasn't big enough for them both with the tension sizzling between them. He'd have to be on guard.

"I don't love Sameer. Not anymore. I think I did at one time, maybe, I don't know. It was something like love, but I'm committed to you. Please. I didn't mean what I said about you staying out of my business. I was being defensive."

"I know. Forget about it."

"Well, if you're not upset about that, then what's got you in a tizzy?"

"You honestly don't know, do you?"

"No. I don't."

"I can't keep my hands off you and if I spend time alone with you, I'm not going to. We need to get out of here, so I can stay on my best behavior."

"What makes you think I want you to keep your hands off me?"

"That's part of the problem. I don't think you'd stop me, so I need to stop myself. I don't want to dishonor God. I also can't stop wondering how much of you wants to move faster, and how much of you simply doesn't trust me not to act the way Sameer did."

"I trust you. I think. And I get the honoring God thing. I've been trying to do that the last couple of years, but you bring out fresh desires in me."

"We can do this. We need to look out for each other and keep a bit of distance. Besides, the Lord knows our hearts, and if we're trying to honor Him, He will give us the strength to do so."

"I want to honor Him." She bit her lower lip before looking away from him. "You know I'm not innocent, right? Before Sameer."

"I know. I've heard about your wild days. They're behind you. Let's look forward."

"Thank you for understanding."

"I'm not perfect either, squirrel. Let's get some grub." He kissed her on the forehead and put the truck in gear.

Chapter 15

The commencement speech was brief. Claudia was happy about that. She didn't want to sit through it and couldn't have recapped it to save her life. She knew it had something to do with bright futures and self-discipline. When her name was called, and she moved forward to receive her diploma, she briefly stopped and smiled for the camera man before descending the steps and making her way back to her seat. After waiting for hundreds of other graduates to get their diplomas, she finally broke free and found Dawson and her family.

There were light refreshments served to celebrate, but she wanted to get out of there and said as much when her father handed her a dozen pink roses still resting in a box. They were lovely. Her mother and sister were both there and gave her a big hug and congratulated her on her accomplishment. Dawson gave her a single red rose, and that made her smile. *Red for love. He must love me.*

They went to a seafood restaurant where her father ordered a steak while the rest of them had lobster. She was blessed to be surrounded by family. Although unsure how she was going to use her degree, she understood that God had a plan for her and that it would come together. It might not be a nice neat perfect life plan, but it would come together one piece at a time. A jigsaw puzzle.

Her eyes met Dawson's across the table and she smiled. She saw something in his eyes that she was afraid to read too much into. "Who's going to help me move into the farmhouse next Saturday?" she asked.

Following a resounding chorus of "I'm busy," they all relented and agreed to help. She'd known they would. Her family always came through for her. And she knew she could count on Dawson.

Stella popped a piece of lobster into her mouth after dipping it in the butter sauce. The butter leaked down her chin and she wiped it with her napkin. "I have something I need your help with too." She surveyed everyone present.

"What's that?" Dawson asked.

"It's a charity thing. I volunteered to share my testimony down at the shelter. They could use more volunteers to dish out food and I could use the moral support. Is anyone up for it?"

They all agreed to go. It wasn't the best neighborhood, so they didn't want Stella down there alone. The tough part was that it was the day after moving day.

Moving day was upon them. Her and Sofie had packed up their apartment and were ready to move out. Sofie was moving back home with her mom. They would start the day with a truckload going there, then return to the apartment to reload the truck and head out to Dushore. Claudia was empowered and ready for a new adventure, but her heart hurt at the thought of being separated from her friend. "I'm going to miss you."

Sofie rolled her eyes. "You're not getting rid of me that easy. We'll still see each other all the time."

Claudia doubted that there was much truth in the statement. She'd seen how people grew apart when no longer in close proximity. "Give me a hug anyhow."

"We're going to be together all day moving this mess." She used her chin to indicate the boxes piled high in their living room.

"Humor me." Claudia wrapped her arms around her friend. "I'm going to have my own place. It will be quiet. You can visit me anytime."

"You have Dawson next door. You may never have a moment to yourself again, my friend. That man will be on your doorstep every day."

"Not every day."

"Every single day. Speak of the cowboy and he rides in in a white pick-up instead of on a white horse."

"Right on time. Let's get this chariot loaded." Claudia picked up a box and headed out the door.

They worked from eight o'clock in the morning until four o'clock in the afternoon. They left Sofie at her mom's house around noon, so she could unpack. She'd tried to go back with them, but they insisted there were more than enough people to move Claudia into the farmhouse.

Dawson suggested they make a pizza run. Claudia convinced him that they should all go into town since there was no way to get pizza back to the farmhouse without it arriving cold.

Her mother had to be dragged out of the house, as she was trying to clean everything to make it perfect for Claudia's first night.

"Enough. Come enjoy fellowship with your family," Claudia said.

"Okay, but don't complain to me when you're scrubbing soap scum tomorrow."

"I think I'll be able to handle it."

Her mom wiped her hands on her apron and followed her downstairs.

They piled into two vehicles and headed into town. It was fun, but by the time they arrived back at the house, Claudia was spent. She was ready for her family to go home. Thankfully, they all headed out shortly after arriving back at the house.

"Call if you need me to come back out here and help you get stuff organized," Joy said.

"Don't call me." Stella grinned as she picked up a sleeping Paul to carry him out to the car.

"I won't need to call anyone. You were all a tremendous help and I'm glad that we got so much done, but I can handle the rest. I need sleep first."

"Did anyone make up the bed?" Joy asked.

"Mom, I've been sleeping out here practically every weekend. The bed is made up. I stopped staying in the garage loft a while ago, I made up the green bedroom and have been staying in there."

"Oh, that room is perfect for you. It's a decent size and has that stone fireplace. Call if you need anything. Anything at all."

"I will, Mom. Love you."

"I love you too. I can't believe you're a college graduate and now you're going to live way out here by yourself."

"She'll be okay, Joy. Let's go home and let her get some rest." Jim said.

Claudia hugged everyone, and they stood in the doorway talking for another fifteen minutes before her family headed home. Dawson came up behind her as she watched them drive away. "You okay?"

"I think so. I'm overwhelmed. So much has changed in the past few days."

"It's going to continue to change, you know."

"I don't know how much more change I can handle." She turned to face him, put both her hands on his chest and gazed up at him.

"I should get going, too. I'll pick you up tomorrow for Stella's charity thing in Wilkes-Barre. We shouldn't spend too much time alone together after dark."

"Are you serious? You stay and watch movies all the time."

"I do. And you have no idea how hard that is for me. It gets more and more difficult to walk away each night. With you living right next door, we should set a few ground rules to protect our commitment to waiting."

"What is it we're waiting for again?"

"You know what we're waiting for. Goodnight, Claudia. I love you."

"You tell me you love me now? As you're walking out of the house?"

"Is there a better time than when I'm ready to say it?"

"I don't know. It's kind of anticlimactic."

"Well, you could've said it back. That would've been the normal thing to do. Instead of jumping all over me about my timing."

"I do, you know," Claudia said.

"You do what?"

"You're going to make me say it?"

"You know I am."

"I love you."

He drew her close and kissed her long and hard before walking out the door and closing it behind him. She turned around and leaned against the door as she waited for his truck to pull away. Sometimes doing the right thing didn't feel good.

Claudia was trying to decide what dress to wear when she heard Dawson holler up the stairs. "You about ready?"

She yelled back. "I'll be down in a minute."

Ten minutes later, she sauntered down the stairs.

"That was a long minute."

She ignored him and followed him to the truck. "Are you sure you don't want to take my car? It's much better on gas than this thing you drive."

"There is not a chance I will be seen driving in a punch buggy. Hop in." He opened the passenger door for her, as usual. She no longer snapped at him or gave him dirty looks when he opened doors for her. She was enjoying being treated like a lady, but she wouldn't tell him that.

After they got a few minutes down the road, he glanced over at her. "I've been thinking."

"That's scary. You should stop that."

"Seriously. I've been thinking that we should go out. On a real date. I haven't taken you out on a date."

"Sure, you have. We went out that night my tire blew. And the following week."

"They weren't dates."

"We went horseback riding."

"That wasn't a date either," he said.

"You've come over for a few movie nights."

"Also, not real dates."

"Well, what did you have in mind?"

"I'm thinking a night out. Dinner and a movie. Nothing elaborate. An actual date. You deserve to be courted properly."

"I would enjoy that," she said.

"Excellent. I would, too."

"Friday night work for you?"

"It's a date. No. Wait. I have drill this weekend. Is the following Friday okay?"

"My parents will be flying into town that day. How about we do this sooner rather than pushing it off. What about this Wednesday?"

"Wednesday works."

"Perfect. I'll pick you up at six."

When they finally arrived at the shelter, Claudia turned to Dawson and raised an eyebrow. "This is a dangerous neighborhood. You're carrying, right?"

"Of course, you?"

"Always."

They hurried into the building. It didn't take long before they were put to work dishing out food. And then helping with the dishes. Stella's testimony was moving. Claudia hadn't realized how much her sister had been through. Sure, she knew most of the story, but many of the details were missing and hearing her speak put everything in perspective and made it seem more real. She hugged her sister afterward and told her how much she loved her and admired her strength of character. Stella shrugged off the compliment and told her it was all God. While unquestionably true, it didn't change Claudia's admiration for her older sister.

Claudia was putting on her makeup, when Dawson shouted up the stairs. "Are you about ready?"

"Yeah. I'll be down in a minute."

She wondered if he was getting tired of waiting for her to get ready every time he picked her up. When she walked downstairs, he was seated in an easy chair. He appeared relaxed with his eyes closed. She overheard him praying. Not an uncommon occurrence for him, but oddly he was praying aloud. He must not know she'd come down. "What was that?" she asked the question to make him aware of her presence.

"Oh, sorry. I was— Nevermind. You look fabulous."

"Thank you. I thought I'd dress up. I don't get many opportunities."

"Much appreciated. Let's head out."

He took her to a classy restaurant that served steak and seafood. She decided to go with a petite filet mignon since she'd had lobster when she went out for her graduation. It was cooked to perfection.

Dawson had ordered prime rib. It looked overcooked to her, but he seemed to enjoy it.

She was stuffed, so Dawson ordered them dessert to go. "We'll surely be hungry again by the time the movie is over, and we get back from the theater. We can eat them at your house."

"I thought you didn't want to be alone with me."

"I think we can control ourselves for a few minutes over dessert. Don't you?"

"I'm not making any promises." She gave him her best seductive smile.

He laughed. "You're too much, girl."

She enjoyed the movie. She would've preferred a romantic comedy, but he had chosen a drama that captivated her attention and made her think. It had a happy ending and that was the main criteria by which she judged movies.

When they arrived at her door that night, Dawson paused. She saw his hesitation and spoke to ease his mind. "I was kidding earlier. I won't try to seduce you. You know that, right?"

"I do. It wasn't you I was worrying about. We can do this. Let's enjoy our dessert." He pushed the door open and then remembered he'd left their food in the truck, so he turned back for it.

She heard a noise at the back of the house and went to investigate. Nothing appeared amiss. Undoubtedly her overactive imagination.

Dawson came in and gave her the cheesecake she'd ordered. It was loaded with strawberries. Yum. He'd gotten carrot cake. Not as delicious as her cheesecake, she'd bet. They sat together at the table long after their food was gone. They reminisced about their pasts and the summers when they intersected. He laughed that he was now dating the bratty girl with the pigtails. She punched him. It was a pleasant night. When he finally stood to go, she regretted seeing him leave.

He was right. They had needed a real date. She now felt more like his girlfriend. It was strange. She'd grown such strong feelings for him. They'd only been seeing each other for a couple of months. She wanted him to hold her. She felt complete when he pulled her into his arms. They stayed that way for several moments.

"Let's do this again next week. Okay?" He peered down at her.

She nodded against his chest. "I'd like that."

He extricated himself from her arms and left her standing there. She wrapped her arms around her middle and stood there until his truck pulled away. Then she trudged up the stairs to prepare for bed.

Wouldn't it be nice if they didn't have to part every night? Maybe one day they'd get married and he wouldn't have to leave. The thought caught her off guard.

Chapter 16

When Claudia pulled into the lot a few minutes before six, she had already been up for hours. She walked quickly and purposefully inside and prepared for first formation. Her fellow Marines were milling around. Many were drinking coffee. A few were on cell phones, but everyone would snap to attention at 0600 hours for formation.

Claudia remained alert, watching for the commanding officer to enter the hall. When she did, she lined up with the others.

She did well on her PT tests. She was surprised she'd kept her time up. She thought she would be lagging since she hadn't been out jogging as often as she liked. Finding that body had seriously messed up her jogging schedule. She'd had to use a treadmill at school and hadn't bought one yet for the house. She hated running indoors.

The rest of the day involved mundane tasks. Her unit needed to be ready for deployment. She didn't take her job lightly. They counted on each other and any one of them could prove vital to another's survival.

She arrived home after drill still dressed in uniform. Pushing through the front door, she tossed her bag aside and sat down to unlace her boots. No sooner had her tush hit the cushion than a knock sounded at the door. She sighed deeply before rising with her boots still in place to answer it.

Seeing Dawson through the window, she opened the door. "You interrupted me taking my boots off. For that you have to pay."

"I think my vision of my lovely Claudia in need of my manly protection has been forever distorted."

"What are you talking about?"

"You look like a Marine."

"I am a Marine."

"I know that. I mean you've told me that. But I've never seen you in uniform and it's weird."

"Wow. You're blunt. Have you lost your mind? You know I'm not a weakling that needs you to fight my battles for me. I prefer having you around to fight them with me, but I don't expect you to be my big, bad protector."

"I know. I want to be your protector though."

"Stop being an idiot and help me get these boots off."

"You want me to go near those stinky feet."

"Oh, shut up and help me."

He knelt in front of her to remove her boots. "See, you do need me. By the way, my mom always told me 'shut up' is a bad word."

"Oh, yeah. I guess I'm cursing at you then. I should fit right in with the other Marines."

"I'll wash your mouth out with soap, young lady." His lips turned up at the corners and his dimple deepened.

After getting the boots off, she pulled out the hair band that was keeping her hair tight to her scalp and shook out her hair.

"Now you look more like my Claudia."

"Oh, now I'm *your* Claudia?"

"Yep. Sure are."

"Then you better get used to me this way. I'm in the Reserves for at least four more years. And that's if I don't re-up."

"I'll get used to it. I could even learn to like it. A little. I just wasn't expecting it. I don't know why. I knew you had drill this weekend, but I'm not used to you not being all feminine."

"Deal with it."

"Yes, Ma'am." He saluted her. "Do you want to come over for cocoa and a movie tonight? I wasn't sure if you'd be up for it after your busy weekend, but if you are, it would make my night. Last chance for alone time at my place. My parents are flying in."

"I know. You mentioned that. Sure, I can come over. Not another drama is it?" Why was he suddenly willing to be alone with her? Was he suspending the 'ground rules'?

"No, it's one of those Christian fiction movies. You usually enjoy those."

She thought about it. Yeah, they had meaningful messages even if the acting sometimes left something to be desired. The Christian labels couldn't always afford to pay the big money that attracted top talent. They were usually low-budget films, but she enjoyed them. They helped her to keep her thoughts and mind pure. Many of the secular movies were far from wholesome.

"I'll see you over there in a half hour or so. I need to take a shower and get changed."

"You mean you're not coming over in military fatigues and combat boots?"

"Keep it up and I might."

He leaned down to kiss her. "I'll see you shortly."

Claudia answered the telephone. "Another one? This is getting out of control."

The officer on the other end of the line responded. "This was out of control with the first body. We have a serial killer on the loose. You're not safe. You should stay around family and friends at all times."

"I'll do that. Thanks for the update. And the warning." She disconnected the call and decided to take a walk over to Dawson's house. He was picking up his parents today, but he would want to know. Not that she was afraid. She could handle one lone serial killer. As the thought went through her head, she knew she was out of her league. This man wasn't sane. He didn't play by the rules.

As she came off the wooded path into the clearing in front of Dawson's place, she scanned the area, looking toward the stables and then the house. He wasn't back yet.

She strolled over to the stables and ran her hand down Snowflakes neck. She enjoyed spending time with the sweet palomino. After nuzzling her for a few minutes, she visited with Huckleberry. Her parents had always insisted she ride gentle mares and geldings. She hadn't been permitted to ride a stallion. She considered taking him out, but decided against it. Saying her goodbyes to the horses, she made her way to the porch and sat on the swing to wait for Dawson and his parents.

They pulled up in Dawson's truck about twenty minutes later. When they made their way up to the porch, Claudia went to help Dawson with the bags. Grabbing the smallest of the bags, she walked toward the front door. Mrs. Montgomery opened it and she set the bag inside. Dawson followed suit.

"Hi, Mr. and Mrs. Montgomery. It's been a long time."

"Claudia McIntyre? Wow. Aren't you a lovely vision? All grown up and more beautiful than ever," Mrs. Montgomery said.

Warmth flooded Claudia's face. "Thank you." She turned to Dawson. "They found another body. The officer who called urged me not to be alone. I'm fine on my own, but I knew if I didn't tell you, you'd go ballistic."

"You're not fine on your own. You're staying here. We'll all go out for a nice dinner to welcome my parents home and then we'll figure out what to do next, okay?"

"You're being bossy."

"If you didn't want that. You wouldn't be here. You knew I would take control of the situation."

"You are such a chauvinist, thinking that because a woman tells you about her problems it means she wants a rescuer. I'm going home."

"Please stay. Come to dinner with us. I promise you my parents would love to have you."

"Fine, but I'm going home as soon as we get back."

"Okay, but promise you'll at least call your father before we go."

"Sure."

Dawson sat at the table in the kitchen with his parents. Claudia was on the phone with her father in the other room.

"Dawson, she's turned into quite the young lady. I know you've been seeing each other. Is it getting serious?" his mother asked.

"Yeah, Mom. It is. I'm going to ask her to marry me."

"Already, are you sure?" His father chimed in.

"I am. She's the one for me. She doesn't know it yet though, so can you keep it to yourself, at least until I think she can handle the idea?"

"Mum's the word," his mother said.

His father nodded in agreement.

He turned on the television. It was time for the 4:30 news. "Let's take a look at the news before we go out."

The first story was about an arrest in Williamsport. They caught the serial killer responsible for the deaths of two students from Legion University and three other victims. "Claudia!" he shouted. "Hurry in here. You've got to see the news."

She spoke into her phone. "Hold on, Dad. Dawson said there is something on the news I have to see."

She stood there staring at the television. The report indicated that Professor Marcus had disfigured and stuffed the body of the twenty-three-year-old victim into a black garbage bag. After several minutes she finally spoke. "I don't believe it. Not Professor Marcus. It can't be him."

He led her to a seat at the table and she put her arms on the table and leaned her head on them. "This can't be true. Sofie's been dating him all year. She hasn't come out and told me, but I've seen them together. She denies it's anything, but it is."

"You can't be serious?"

"I am."

"We've got to call her before she sees it on the news."

"If she hasn't already." She picked the cordless phone back up and heard her father's voice. "Dad. I forgot you were on there. I'm sorry. They think they caught him, but they have to have the wrong man. They arrested my art professor. He's a gentle giant. It can't be him. He's been dating Sofie. I've got to call her. It's a long story. I'll fill you in later."

She dialed Sofie and she picked up on the first ring.

"Did you see the news?"

"I saw it. It isn't true. He called me a short time ago to see if I wanted to come over for grilled fish."

"Do you want us to pick you up?"

"No. I'll be okay."

"You shouldn't be alone. Maybe we can help."

Dawson paced back and forth in the kitchen. "If she isn't willing to let us come down there, then there's not much more we can do."

"I know."

"Now that they have someone in custody, they can compare the DNA found on the tire and under the fingernails to him."

"Yeah. I guess. I hope it doesn't match. As much as I want this to be over, I don't want it to be him."

"Should we head out to dinner? I know it sounds callous, but we have to eat, and she doesn't want us there for moral support."

He glanced at his parents, who nodded their agreement.

Claudia rubbed her neck. "Yes. Let's go have dinner. I'm going to head down there after dinner, whether she wants my company or not. I think you should stay here with your parents."

"I'm coming with you."

"She's more likely to talk to me if I'm by myself. You know how tight-lipped she can be."

"I don't like it."

"I know."

Dawson wondered what his parents thought of coming home to this drama. They loaded into his truck to head into town.

Claudia put her hand over Sofie's and remained silent. Eventually, if she kept her mouth shut, Sofie would start talking. She'd learned to understand how to get her friend to share.

It took more than twenty minutes of waiting, but Sofie finally broke the silence. "Please tell me this isn't happening. I finally find a man who is interested in me, and he turns out to be a serial killer. I won't believe it. It can't be true. Can it?"

"I don't believe it either."

"This is so hard." She stood and walked to the window. "I'm not sure I can do this."

"What can't you do?"

"Tell the truth."

"You're going to need to elaborate."

"When I stay over, he leaves during the night. If I tell the cops that, they're going to think he's guilty. I don't think he is, but I don't know where he goes."

"I thought you two broke up? When did you get back together?"

"I may not have mentioned it, but you knew we'd made up."

"Well, sure. I figured."

Sofie walked to the bottom of the steps and hollered up. "Ma, I'm going out!"

She grabbed her keys and her purse and headed toward the door. "You joining me?"

"Of course. Where are we going?"

"Back to Williamsport. I'm going to the station."

Claudia snatched the keys. "You shouldn't be driving as upset as you are. I'll drive."

She was surprised that Sofie brokered no argument. Her friend must be more distraught than she'd originally realized.

Sofie walked up to the desk and inquired whether she could speak to the officer handling the case. A receptionist led them to a windowless room where they waited for the officer.

A man walked through the door closing it behind him. "I'm Detective Griffith. You've saved me a bit of trouble, Sofie."

"How's that?"

"We were about to track you down to verify Johan Marcus' story. He claims he was with you until about ten o'clock last night."

"Yes, we were together."

"What were you doing?"

"We had pizza and then talked until we got in an argument. Then I drove home."

"Where's home now that school is over?"

"I'm back at my mom's house in Lopez."

"That's a considerable distance from here for you to show up at the station this quickly."

"I saw the news and wondered if I could help in any way. I couldn't sit home wondering what was going on. He didn't do this, you know?"

"Actually, no. I don't know that. His fingerprints are in the sap on a tree beside where the body was found."

"That's circumstantial at best," Claudia said.

Yet, it did sound incriminating. Maybe he did do this? Could he be guilty? Claudia's mind raced over all the times she'd been alone with Professor Marcus in the art studio. They'd even spent time together outside of class. Nothing inappropriate. He couldn't be the person trying to destroy her life. Could he?

"That may be so, but we'll be holding him while we put together our case. He still had the sap on his fingers when we picked him up. It was fresh. We think he dumped the body this afternoon. We have to put together the pieces of the puzzle, so that we can nail him."

"You sound as if he's already convicted in your mind," Sofie said.

"Some cases are open and shut. This looks like one of them."

"He told you he was there because he was fishing. Aren't you concerned that you could have the wrong guy?" Claudia asked.

"Not at all. We have our guy."

"Did you compare his DNA to what you found under the fingernails of the other victims?" Sofie asked.

"If it doesn't match, it doesn't matter. This is a separate murder. He could have killed this woman and not killed the others."

"But—"

"Do yourself a favor and let this go. Your boyfriend is guilty." The detective stood up and strode from the room.

Chapter 17

*D*awson cut the long stems off some sunflowers from along the fence. The sun shined brightly there and grew lovely flowers. He couldn't wait to give them to Claudia. They were her favorite. He watched a bee buzzing around and smiled at the beauty of God's creation. *Thank you, Lord. For all of this.*

After his brief prayer, Dawson mounted Huckleberry and headed next door. Claudia was with her family in Edinsville, but she was planning to come meet him afterward for date night. He had something special planned. He put his horse in the stables at the McIntyre residence and hurried inside. He'd collected petals from the sunflowers, and he scattered them in a path for her to follow. The path led to the deck where he'd set the table with a white linen table cloth, put a vase with sunflowers in the center of the table, and set out the fine china. He made a meal of shrimp and scallops sautéed and served over linguini. He even made dessert, a simple apple tart that he planned to serve with ice cream.

He was nervous. He wanted everything to be perfect for her. As he set the fire in the chimenea he thought over his plans and went over every detail in his mind, hoping he hadn't forgotten anything. She would be back soon. He sat down at the table and waited.

It wouldn't be long before she arrived.

The day had been long and hard. She'd been helping at her parents' house. They'd thrown an anniversary party for Pastor Mark and his wife. Everyone had fun. It was a satisfied exhaustion that enveloped her. A job well done. She smiled as she drove toward Dushore. The hill up Route 487 was always scary in the winter, but now that summer was here the ride was enjoyable. She saw two doe with a fawn on one side of the road and shortly after a family of possums on the other side of the road. As she passed Ricketts Glen State Park, she thought about the waterfall trail and how much she'd liked to go there as a child. She didn't relish hiking the whole trail. Way too stren-uous. Seven miles round trip on rough terrain. That was Stella's territory. She liked the shorter trail. It was flat. And it led directly to the tallest waterfall. She could sit there for hours, people watching as the tourists hiked up and down the waterfall trail. Few of them took the other trail, so her walk back to the car was relaxing and calm.

She wondered if Dawson would want to come out here with her. He would want to hike the whole trail. He liked to give his all to everything he did. Would she be able to be with a man that intense? She shook her head and dismissed the thought outright. He was an exemplary man and he cared about her. Why was she stressing over a few personality quirks and what they could mean for their future?

Her thoughts continued to ping pong between Dawson and other areas of her life, but they always ended up back on him. Why? The excitement at seeing him contin-ued to build until she finally pulled up outside the farmhouse. He was already there, she could see smoke coming up behind the house. She walked around the outside of the house to the back patio and found Dawson waiting for her there, the table set beautifully with a vase of sunflowers in the center.

He jumped from his seat. "You were supposed to come through the house."

"Why?"

"You just were, but this will have to do."

"I can go back around, if you want me to."

"No. It's fine. Come here."

He pulled her into his arms and hugged her tight for a moment. Sometimes she wished he would hold her longer, but she knew that the brief encounters were an exer-cise in self-control for him, and that he wanted to protect her. He knew she wasn't inno-cent, they'd talked about their pasts, but he was determined to treat her like a lady. Whether she wanted him to or not. A moan of frustration escaped.

He peered down at her as he held her arm's length away. "What was that?"

"Nothing. What's for dinner, it smells like seafood and garlic. Yum."

"I hope it tastes as good as it smells. We're having sautéed scallops and shrimp over linguine. Give me a minute and I'll bring it out." He pulled her chair out for her.

"This is delicious." She said it before he sat down.

"What are you doing eating? We didn't pray yet." He raised an eyebrow, before sliding into his chair and bowing his head. "Thank you, Lord, for the food you've pro-vided. Please bless it to our bodies. I ask your continued protection and preservation for us. Please lead us in your ways."

"Amen. Let's eat." She smiled at him and then devoured her food. "Wow. That was delicious. I don't think I had time to eat much of anything today. I was back and forth cooking and serving food, but I only picked at a few things in the kitchen. Somehow, you knew exactly what I would need." She was stuffed.

"We still have dessert."

"That might have to wait a while. I'm going to burst."

"How about a walk?" She held her hand out to him and he helped her up. They strolled around the property until they came to a secluded spot where he used to have a fort that she would always sneak up on when she wanted to spy on him. The old fort was fallen down, but she could still see where it had been.

"Do you remember when you used to come out here and spy on me?"

"How did you know? I was quiet."

"I always knew when you and your sister were sneaking around these woods. You thought you were quiet, but you made more noise than a pair of squirrels chasing each other through autumn leaves."

"Stealth spies, huh?"

"You know it." He reached into his back pocket and pulled out a box.

Panic welled up inside her as he got down to one knee. This was what she wanted, wasn't it?

He held out the box. "Claudia, will you marry me?"

"Um."

He rose to his feet and towered over her. He gently whispered into her ear. "What do you mean 'um'?"

"Um. You caught me by surprise. I wasn't expecting this."

"It's okay. You don't have to say anything. You can think about it." She wanted to shout yes, but she couldn't get the word to come out. What was wrong with her? He took her hand and they walked back toward the house. Her heart was beating rapidly and the heat in her face told her she was beet red. She wanted to say yes, so they could get on with celebrating the start of their lives together, but she couldn't spit the word out.

They got back to the house and sat together on the love seat to watch a movie. Guilt ate her alive when she'd seen the trail of petals going out to the patio. He'd gone to a lot of trouble to make this night perfect and she'd gone and messed everything up. She rested her head against his shoulder and settled in to watch a romantic comedy. He hated romantic comedies. Another kindness. He was practically perfect.

Stella answered on the fourth ring. "Hello."

"I thought you were going to let me go to voicemail."

"It's hectic here as always, but I always have time for you. What's up?"

"Dawson asked me to marry him."

"Oh my. I can't wait. What will I wear to the wedding?"

"If I were getting married, you would be my maid of honor and wouldn't need to figure out what to wear, but I didn't say yes, Stella."

"What do you mean, you didn't say yes? You love him, don't you?"

"Yes. I do."

"Then why didn't you say yes?"

"I don't know. I couldn't say anything. I froze up. I wish I could explain it, but I can't."

"Well, you'd better straighten this out quickly. Now that you live there, you'll be seeing him whether you want to or not. You had best decide if he is the one, and if he isn't you might want to talk to Dad about moving back home."

"Of course, he's the one. I wouldn't have moved out here if he wasn't. I panicked. I'll straighten it out. If he lets me. Do you think I hurt him?"

"Absolutely. What do you think? How would you feel if the situation were reversed?"

"Awful. Just terrible."

"Claudia this isn't something you can let simmer. Why don't you go over there now?"

"It's way too late. Besides if I creep through the woods at this time of night, he might shoot at me."

"You could try calling first. Or driving."

"Yes, I could. I think I want to wait until morning."

"It's your life, but I wouldn't wait too long. Men like Dawson aren't easy to come by. He's totally in love with you. You don't want to give that up, do you?"

"No, of course not. He's the best. I'm an idiot."

"I didn't say you're an idiot."

"You didn't have to. I got the drift. Look, I'm going to go. I have to think about this."

"I'm sorry. I didn't mean to sound so harsh. Maybe you should pray about it."

"I will. I'll call you tomorrow." Claudia disconnected the telephone without saying her usual 'I love you.' She did, of course, but she didn't want to say the words. She ran a hot bubble bath and laid out her pajamas. It might be summer, but to her a hot bath always felt soothing. Her mind was running overtime and she needed to find a way to relax.

Claudia curled her hair with an ancient curling iron. It was covered in nasty baked-on hair spray, so she didn't want it in her hair, but today her hair wouldn't do a thing with the blow dryer. It was at that in-between stage. She'd been growing it out and now that her hair was longer than shoulder length, it was unmanageable. Stella would strangle her if she heard her complaining about her straight hair and its flyaways. She struggled to keep her curls controlled so much of the time, that she didn't believe people with straight hair had hair troubles.

Giving up after adding a few curls to the ends and front, she unplugged the iron. She wondered if she would see Dawson today. He had to be hurt after her avoidance of his question last night. Why couldn't she have said yes? She wanted to, but the words weren't coming. Even now, she should be running over there and telling him how much she loved him and how she'd made a mistake in not throwing herself in his arms last night and agreeing to marry him. That was what she wanted, wasn't it? It would bring her the most happiness. She should marry Dawson. So, why was she hesitating? It wasn't Sameer. Maybe it was the fear of betrayal that had been brought on by Sameer, but it definitely wasn't lingering feelings for him. Fear wasn't from God. She remembered the verse, she'd been forced to memorize it in school. It was in Second Timothy. "For God hath not given us the spirit of fear; but of power, and of love, and of a sound mind." A sound mind. She could use one of those.

What was she doing here messing with her hair? It was time to find Dawson and make things right.

She hurried to get dressed and on her way out the door, she ran into him. Literally. He had to hold her up to keep her from falling. "Where are you going in such a hurry?" he asked.

"To see you."

"Where's the fire?"

"I had to tell you that I'm sorry."

"You decided to say no then? It's okay. I thought that might be your answer after your reaction last night."

"No—"

"You don't have to say anything. It's okay. I understand."

"Stop talking. Please. I'm trying to say yes. I want to marry you. I wanted to say yes last night, but the word wouldn't come past my lips. Yes, I want to marry you. Yes, I want to spend the rest of my life with you. Yes. Yes. Yes."

"Are you sure? I don't want to pressure you."

"I'm positive." She threw herself back into his arms and he held her close. Reaching into his pocket he pulled out the ring. "I brought it back with me. Just in case."

Her tears flowed.

"Why are you crying? I thought you said you wanted this?"

"I do." She wiped away her tears.

"Then why are you crying?"

"I guess because I'm happy."

"Women."

"Don't start that already."

They both laughed, and he picked her up and spun her around, laughter crinkling the corners of his eyes.

"I have to call my parents. And Stella. And Sofie."

"Can we enjoy this for a few minutes? Just the two of us?"

"Sounds heavenly." He placed the ring on her finger. She turned her hand watching as rainbow prisms shined in the princess-cut diamond.

He kissed her gently. "Let's plan for fall wedding. I don't want to wait any longer than necessary to make you my wife."

The shrill ring of the telephone interrupted the moment.

Claudia answered the telephone after glancing at the caller ID. "Hey, Dad. Wait. What? Slow down and say that again." She paused for a moment glancing at Dawson and signaling with her hands that she wanted him to get the keys. She grabbed her purse and jacket from the hook. "We're leaving now. It'll take us about an hour to get there." She disconnected the call.

"Mom is in the hospital. She's being taken into surgery now. Jason is at work, so Stella doesn't have a sitter. I'm going to go to the hospital now and sit with Dad. Do you want to drive with me, or stay here?"

"I'm coming with you, of course. What's wrong with your mom? Why does she need surgery?"

They hurried out to Dawson's truck. "They aren't sure. Dad said she's in extreme pain. They did a CT scan and they can see that she's a mess inside, but they can't tell for sure what the issue is. They're going to do exploratory surgery. I don't know why he didn't call sooner. It sounds like they've been at the hospital for hours." Dawson closed her door as she finished the sentence.

He got in the truck. "If Stella wants, I can watch the kids, so she can join you guys too, but that might take a while for me to get you to Danville and then drive back to Edinsville to get the kids."

"Maybe she could meet us at the hospital with the kids and you could drive them back home later when it's time to put them to bed? I'll call her on the way and we can work it out. If I know Jason as well as I think I do, he'll be on his way home before we need to worry about it."

"You're probably right."

Claudia made the call to Stella. They planned to meet at the hospital. Stella was going to bring the kids with her and figure out what to do when it came near their bedtime. Claudia offered Dawson's services, but Stella said she didn't know yet if he would be needed. After all, Mom would probably be out of surgery and then she could go back home with the boys.

Chapter 18

Jim stood when Claudia entered the waiting room door. He shook his head. Tears filled his eyes. Claudia put her arm around him and walked him over to a nearby bank of chairs. "No, Daddy, it can't be." The tears streaming down her face and onto her neck were cold from the air conditioning, but she didn't wipe them away. Her dad didn't volunteer details. She wasn't sure she was ready to hear them.

She hugged her father tightly and cried with him. It was the first time she'd seen him shed tears. He'd told her he'd cried when Stella was abducted, but she hadn't seen him.

Suddenly the realization that she wouldn't see her mother again in this life hit her. The sobs racked her body and she pulled away from her father and pulled her knees to her chest. Her vibrant mother, always so full of life. Why? Death took people away that didn't deserve to die. Why did horrible people get to live and wonderful people like her mother have to die?

Her father had been through this before. He didn't deserve to lose another wife. She wouldn't have been born if her father's first wife had lived.

After a long while, her father finally gave her the details. He stood when he saw Stella come in. "Tell her. I'll be back soon. I need a minute."

Claudia nodded up at him. She wiped her eyes and met her sister's gaze.

Claudia watched as Stella stood straighter, pushing her shoulders back and lifting her chin. She had the kids with her. As Claudia walked over, Stella handed Dawson one of the boys. "Do you think you can carry them both?"

"Sure." She settled the other kid on his hip. Claudia wanted to find humor in the spectacle of Dawson trying to juggle two cranky babies, but she was empty inside.

She glanced down at the shiny diamond decorating her left hand. This should be the happiest time in her life, but how could she walk down the aisle without her mother there to watch her. These were thoughts that needed to be put aside for another time.

It didn't feel real. She watched as Dawson settled the two boys on his lap. Glen stood beside him. Dawson reached over to the table and grabbed a kid's book. Joy was a children's book author. The thought made her start crying again.

He read to the children making the voices of the animals in the book. She wondered where he'd acquired the skill to read books like that, but her thoughts were interrupted when her sister put her arms around her. "Claudia, what's going on?"

"She's gone, Stella. She's gone."

"I thought so after seeing your face. What happened?" She nodded toward their father who had walked across the room and was staring out the door into the hallway. "Did Dad tell you what happened?"

"He said the doctor came out and said that they'd lost her. They did everything they could, but they weren't able to bring her back."

"Why had she needed surgery?"

"When they opened her up, they realized she'd had a bowel rupture. They tried to save her, but she was too far gone. Sepsis. Shock. She didn't get here soon enough. They lost her a few minutes into the surgery. Dad didn't call because he didn't want us driving after receiving the news."

Stella silently wiped away her tears. "I have to tell Glen, Paul, and Cole that their grandmother is gone."

"Don't you think you should wait for Jason to get home from work? Maybe he can get off tomorrow and you can talk to the kids then?"

"And why do I tell them I'm so upset now?" Stella asked with a hint of agitation in her voice.

"I'm sorry, you're right."

"Jason called while I was driving over. He was leaving work. He should be here within half an hour. I can wait until he gets here to tell them. I'm not thinking straight."

Claudia put her arms around her sister and they held each other for several minutes.

"It doesn't seem real," Claudia said.

"No. It doesn't. I keep thinking she is going to walk into the room and tell us it was all a big joke."

"Mom wouldn't joke about something like this."

"No. She certainly wouldn't."

"Stella, I'm sorry about yesterday."

"What do you mean?"

"On the phone. I shouldn't have hung up mad. Especially without telling you I love you."

"Hey, don't worry about it. I know you love me," Stella said. "We've got enough emotional trauma to deal with without worrying about a minor phone spat."

"You've got that right. Look at Dad. I don't know how he's going to get through this."

"He will. His relationship with God will bring him through."

"That sounds so cliché, you know."

"I know it does. But you know it's true. I never would've survived that ordeal a couple of years ago if it wasn't for my relationship with God. You never would've survived this past few months of running from a serial killer if the Lord didn't give you the strength."

"True. Yet, this is so different. It's too much."

Dawson watched as Jim finally walked over and hugged his firstborn. They broke down in each other's arms.

He felt helpless. He rummaged around the stacks of magazines and books for a few minutes and found coloring books. No crayons. Giving up on the coloring books, he changed the television station to Nickelodeon hoping it would keep their minds occupied, so they would be less aware of the angst around them.

It wasn't long before Jason trudged through the door, looking spent from work. Dawson hurried over to him and explained what was happening. Jason's eyes filled when he heard the news. "Has anyone told the kids?"

"No. I think your wife was waiting for you to arrive before breaking it to them."

"She was probably right to do that. We should go home and tell them."

"I imagine Jim will want the whole family around him tonight. Do you think I could swing by your place and get the kids' stuff to take to their house?"

"Oh. There are extras of everything they need already at their grandparents' house, I'm sure it will be fine to go directly there. You're absolutely correct. He won't want to be alone. Are you going to stick around?"

"I am. I couldn't leave Claudia at a time like this."

"Thank you for coming. And for staying. It means a lot to me. As I'm sure it does to Jim and Claudia also."

The family crowded into the kitchen at Jim's house. Claudia rummaged around the kitchen preparing food while Stella and Jason sat on the bar stools at the counter and Jim and Dawson sat at the table. Jim had his head leaned against the back of the chair. Claudia could tell that they were in shock. It wouldn't fully hit them for a couple of days and then the impact would be unbearable. She didn't understand the phenomenon of shock, but she had been through it when her grandfather passed on to his heavenly reward. As she was cutting a plate of brownies to put on the table, Stella noticed the ring. "I see you said yes."

"I did."

"Did you tell Dad yet?" Stella whispered.

"It didn't seem like the appropriate time. Maybe I should take the ring off until it's a better time."

"That doesn't sound smart. How would it make Dawson feel?"

"You're right. I'll leave it on."

"Just wait for Dad to notice it on his own, or if you'd prefer, tell him. He'll still be happy for you."

"I know. I was celebrating my brand-new engagement a few hours ago, and here I am mourning my mother. I can't believe this is happening."

"It isn't fair. Life rarely is." She came around the counter and hugged Claudia.

"I'm not sure I've ever cried this much in my life."

"It's okay. You'll cry a lot more. We both will."

"I think I need to cook something, too. I need to do something to keep me busy and you know this house is going to be teeming with church family soon."

"Did anyone make phone calls yet?" Claudia asked, directing the question to the whole room.

"No, sweetie. I wasn't up to it yet. You can call my secretary if you want. She'll let everyone know. Ask them to stay away until tomorrow."

"Okay, Dad. I'll do that. What about Grandma?" She regretted asking. She didn't want to talk to her dad's secretary. She didn't want to talk to anybody right now, present company excluded.

"I called your grandmother from the hospital. She's devastated. Nobody should ever have to bury their child." Jim's gaze settled on each of his daughters in turn.

"You'd better give Sofie a call, too. She'll never forgive you if you don't let her know what's going on," Stella said.

"I'll call her for you," Dawson said.

Relief flooded through her. She gave him a weak smile and nodded her head, handing him her cell phone. "Thank you. You're the best."

He walked into the other room to make the call. She appreciated his kindness.

Stella tapped a pen open on the counter and opened a notebook. "We need to discuss arrangements."

"Already?" Claudia said.

"We're all together now. And it may be harder to do this later after the initial shock wears off and we're trying to peel ourselves from our beds."

"Your sister is right. I've been through this before. We need to decide on what to do now."

"Let's start with the easy stuff. Did Mom have any plans already set for her funeral? Did she ever say what she wanted?" Stella asked.

"She said she wanted "Amazing Grace" sung. And she asked for a bagpiper to play it as everyone left the church. I don't remember her ever mentioning any other particulars," Jim said.

"Okay. That is doable. We can, at least, make sure Mom's wishes are honored." Claudia sighed. "What about her clothes? What are we going to give the funeral home to dress her in?"

"I think she would want her teal dress. She always looked sharp in it. It was her favorite," Stella said.

They continued to discuss arrangements until Dawson came back in the room.

They'd covered all the basics. Stella would get Mom's clothes together. Claudia would prepare the music. Jim would talk to the funeral director and let him know what they'd decided for everything. Stella picked up the telephone and called the church secretary. Once again Claudia was relieved. How did Stella know that she couldn't handle that yet?

Claudia faced the makeup mirror on the dresser of her childhood bedroom and carefully applied waterproof mascara. Sofie sat on the edge of the bed, already dressed in a floor-length black skirt and dark green dress shirt. Her shoulder-length hair was combed back into a neat bun in the back of her head.

"Want mascara?" Claudia asked.

"You know I don't wear makeup."

"Well, it wouldn't hurt you to wear it from time to time. You look so severe with that librarian's outfit and hairdo. You even have librarian glasses."

Sofie put her head down and stared at her hands.

Claudia palmed herself in the forehead. "I'm sorry. I shouldn't have said that. I'm agitated today."

"I know. And for an understandable reason. Otherwise, I would've punched you in the mouth."

"Sorry. I can't believe I'm going to my mother's funeral. It doesn't seem real. She can't be gone, can she?"

Sofie didn't say anything, but she rose to her feet and put her arm around her friend.

"Sofie, I can't do this. I'm going to be sick."

"You can do this. And you will do this. You are stronger than you know. Moments like this show us how strong we are. Put your shoes on and get your purse. We need to get downstairs."

"Shoes. Oh, no. I don't know what shoes I'm going to wear. I didn't bring any with me from home. I'm sure you have shoes here. I don't have anything appropriate. I could wear a pair of Mom's shoes, but that would be weird."

"You're going to have to wear your mother's shoes. You don't have any time to go into town to buy a pair or drive to Dushore to get yours. I'll go find you appropriate shoes."

"No. I'll do it. I'm not ready for anyone else to touch Mom's stuff."

"Oh. Okay."

"Do you want me to come with you?"

"Would you mind waiting here? Give me one minute."

"Sure."

Claudia walked down the hall to the master bedroom and paused at the door. She took a deep breath and steeled herself to go inside. She stepped through the door and surveyed the room. Everything was the same. Something in her expected the room to look different. It didn't. Her mother's white leather Bible sat on her nightstand as always. Her slippers were stuck half under the edge of the bed. Her comb-and-brush set were still in their usual place on the bureau.

Claudia walked to the big walk-in closet and opened the door. Inside, she found a pair of black high heels that would go well with her suit. They were slightly tight. She usually wore a six and a half. Her mother wore a six. They fit well enough. They would stretch as the day wore on. It's not like her mother would need them back. The thought struck her as cold. She walked to the window and peered out at the stables. What she would give to be back out there with her mother at her side, both of them brushing their horses. "Mom, I miss you already." She whispered the words and a tear escaped her eye before she could brush it away.

Hurrying back down the hall, she stuck her head in her bedroom. "I'm ready, Sofie. Let's head down."

Chapter 19

Claudia sat in the front row of the church with her sister on one side and Dawson on the other. Jason sat behind them with the children. Her father, who was seated beside Stella, sat there stoically as the youth pastor started the service. Claudia didn't register anything he said. He then called for her to come up and say a few words. She stood and walked to the podium, her knees were squishy jellyfish ready to give out on her. Her prepared words were written out neatly on a sheet of notebook paper. She carried it up with her, but the paper was useless, the words blurred on the page. She wouldn't be reading today.

"Hello. I had a few words prepared to read to you, but I can't see the page, so I'll speak from my heart. My mother is the best mother a girl could ask for. I say 'is' rather than 'was,' because my mother has eternal life. She may have left her physical body behind, but she isn't gone. Someday, I'll see her again, I look forward to being with Mom again in New Jerusalem.

"Mom showered us with love our whole lives. She always put her children and her husband's needs before her own. Never did she complain about staying up to help us with a last-minute school project that we procrastinated completing. She put her heart and soul into raising her children and loving her husband. She was able to accomplish so much because of the strength she found in the Lord. Many of you know that Mom wrote children's books and women's devotionals. So, her carefully penned words are ours to keep. Her love for Jesus came out in everything she wrote as well as in all she did and said. She had a passion for seeing souls saved, and she would be disappointed if my father didn't share the salvation message at her funeral. I know he plans to do so.

"Most of you know my older sister, Stella. She declined to speak today. She didn't think she could clearly communicate what needed to be said, but she asked me to tell you that our mother was always an inspiration to her. She was a woman who not only read the words in the Bible and shared them, but lived what it said. She inspired both of us girls to grow closer to God and to trust in His word. Stella is going to try to sing Mom's favorite song."

Claudia made her way to the piano as Stella moved to take the microphone from the podium. The notes of "Amazing Grace" filled the room. When they finished, Claudia made her way back to the front pew as her father made his way to the podium.

He expounded on Romans 10:10 and explained that if anyone in the room wanted to see her mom again, all they had to do was believe in their hearts that Jesus Christ had shed His blood for their sins on the cross. It was that simple. Believe. He shared Ephesians 2:8-9 to show those present that salvation was God's gift and that man could not add to it.

The message took about ten minutes. He shared a personal testimony of how he had met Joy during a low point in his life when his first wife died, and he was lost and overwhelmed. He'd shared how the Lord had placed her in his life to help him through the darkest time of his life and to help redirect his eyes to the Lord. And that she was a constant tangible reminder of God's love and he would miss her greatly.

He remained stoic, not allowing a single tear to fall. The youth pastor, Mark, made his way to the front of the church, and her dad joined her and her sister in the pew.

After a few more words, he had everyone turn to the hymn "Blessed Assurance." His rich, sonorous voice was comforting to Claudia as she listened to the words of the timeless hymn.

Dawson held Claudia's hand as they walked across the muddy expanse that was the cemetery. Jim had shared his thoughts on his wife's eternal destination and his joy at her being with the Lord. He got down and sat in the front row leaving the closing of the service to the church's youth pastor, Mark. The younger man had led the bereaved in a closing song and it had touched Dawson's heart. He'd never considered the words to "Blessed Assurance" before the service, but now that he had, he knew that the words would forever be carved on his heart. How blessed they were to be assured of their salvation and eternal security to know that Jesus would remain their Savior no matter what happened. How sweet it was to be sealed with the Holy Spirit of promise.

He glanced down at Claudia who was trying to wipe mud from her high heel. He gave her a weak smile and squeezed her hand. It was going to be one of the hardest days of her life. He hadn't lost a parent, but he somehow knew that there could be no greater personal loss other than the loss of a child. Jason talked with him about his experience losing both of his parents and his brother. It had been painful to hear about. He couldn't imagine what it must've been like for him. The best thing he could do for Claudia was to be there for her. To give her the love and support she needed.

"I'm not sure I can do this. I can handle it when terrible things happen to me, but I'm not sure I can handle never seeing my mom again in this life. I'm drowning in sorrow. I'm not sure I'll ever reach the surface again to take a breath of fresh air."

"You can do this. We'll just be here for a few minutes before we move on and go to the luncheon. You can't think in terms of forever. Get through the next five minutes. When that is over, then you can concentrate on the following five minutes. It will be five minutes at a time today. Maybe next week, you'll be strong enough to get through ten minutes at a time, but today, focus on getting through the next five minutes. And remember you will see her again."

"I'll try."

He guided her into one of the few chairs set close to the casket. Her father and Stella already occupied two of the others. He indicated that he would be standing behind her as he gestured for Joy's mother to be seated beside her granddaughter.

When the sobbing began, he had tissues handy. He wasn't sure he had brought enough for all the ladies who were crying. Gratitude filled him as he saw Jason reach in his pocket and hand Stella a few tissues. Jason, of course, knew how to be prepared for such a difficult occasion. Sadly, he was no stranger to funerals. Dawson hadn't lost anyone since his grandparents. His parents were getting up in years, but were both healthy. He had no siblings and minimal extended family, an aunt and uncle and a few cousins.

Dawson brought his attention back to the words that Pastor Mark was speaking. The girls got up and laid the roses they'd been given on top of the coffin. The men laid carnations down and soon the top of the coffin was no longer visible for all the flowers. The turnout had been high. Could one say that of a funeral or was it disrespectful? He wasn't sure, but, nevertheless, they had needed to line the aisles with extra chairs to accommodate the visitors at the church and the crowd that had followed to the cemetery was surprisingly large. He wondered if any of the visitors were her readers. He was sure some had been from her hometown. She'd been a special woman and if the number of people in attendance were any indication, she would be sorely missed.

Putting his arm around Claudia, he walked her back to the car. Now she would need to get through the luncheon. She quit drinking a couple of years earlier, otherwise he might've considered offering her a shot of whiskey to calm her nerves. He knew alcohol was never the solution, but seeing her in so much pain was torture. All he could do was provide her his strength. His love. His comfort. And remind her that the Lord would see her through this.

Claudia sat in the back of the limousine between Dawson and her father. They were on their way to the luncheon. She didn't understand the point in having fancy cars and ostentatious parties to celebrate one's departing from life. Why didn't people celebrate each other's lives while they were still around to hear all the kind things people had to say about them? She supposed it would be bad for prideful people. Get them more puffed up, but her mother could've handled knowing how loved she was.

"Claudia, are you okay?" Dawson whispered.

She must look a wreck. People wouldn't stop asking her if she was okay. Of course, she wasn't. Her mother was dead. Never coming back. Life would never be the same. To Dawson, she gave the slightest head shake to indicate that she was not all right. But he already knew that. She hoped he wouldn't give her any more platitudes about how God would get her through. It was true. Accurate. But, at this moment, she didn't want to hear it. God had let her mother be taken from her. She hadn't even had the chance to tell her that she was engaged to be married. Her body shook with sobs and her father pulled her to him and held her tightly.

"Daddy, I can't do this. I want to go home."

"Sure, honey. If you want to go home, I'll have the driver take you there. You can come out when you're ready."

"No. I'm going to come with you. I don't want you to have to face all those people alone and Stella will be busy with the kids."

"Okay, honey. Whatever you think is best."

They pulled up at the curb in front of the fancy restaurant. Claudia couldn't remember the name of the place. Why hadn't they had everyone come to the house? It would've made so much more sense. Then she considered the cooking and cleaning involved and realized her father had made the right call. This way, when they left here, they could go home and be together without worrying about what more needed to be done.

Dawson walked in the front door of the McIntyre farmhouse. "Claudia, haven't we talked about keeping the door locked?" He asked when he found her in the living room.

"A few times, yes, but what does it matter now? Professor Marcus is in prison."

"I'd feel better if you'd keep the door locked."

"Fine, Dad, I'll keep it locked."

"Not funny," Dawson said.

She wasn't smiling. He sat down beside her and pulled her to him. She buried her head in his shoulder. For a long time, he sat there holding her. He had no idea how to comfort her. He'd never lost a parent, so this was new to him. He was mourning Joy's loss himself, but the depth of Claudia's sorrow wasn't something he could compare to his own. He wanted nothing more than to ease her pain.

"You're looking thin. When was the last time you ate a real meal?"

"I don't know."

"How about we go out for dinner?"

"I don't feel up to it."

"Okay. I'll cook, instead. What would you like?"

"I'm not hungry."

"You have to eat. How about pork chops and macaroni and cheese?"

"Sure. That's fine," she said.

Forty-five minutes later, they were seated at the kitchen table. He said grace and ate his dinner. She took a few bites, but mostly ignored her food.

"I give up. I don't know how to get you to eat," Dawson said.

"I'll eat when I'm hungry."

He gave her a pointed look.

"I'm trying to bounce back. I really am. This is the most painful thing I've ever been through. I can't snap my fingers and turn back into my old self."

"I'm not asking you to."

"It feels like you are."

"I want to be there for you. I don't know how to do that without pushing you away."

Claudia rose from her seat and walked over to his chair putting her arms around him from behind. "I love you and knowing you love me is enough."

"Okay. I'll try not to push so hard."

Mourning wasn't something Claudia had ever fully understood until she lost her mother. It had been months and she was barely able to get out of bed in the morning. Dawson had come over and tried to get her to show an interest in something, but she couldn't bring herself to do much. She'd lost ten pounds and recognized that she needed to take better care of herself.

The bodies had stopped piling up since Professor Marcus had been arrested. It was hard to believe it had been him all along, but she had to accept it.

Today she was making her first real attempt to rejoin the land of the living.

"Hurry up, would you?" she said.

"Where are we going?" Dawson asked.

"You'll see."

She tugged him along the path through the woods to one of her favorite places. She hoped he would enjoy it as much as she did. She'd had him park at the trail head, for the Old Beaver Dam Road Trail, but there was no sign there that indicated what lay at the end, so she expected it would be a surprise to him. Leaves covered the path and the autumn colors were spectacular. As they approached the end of the trail, she covered his eyes before they walked around the last bend. She could hear the crashing of the water, and knew he'd be able to tell where they were going, but it was something that needed to be seen to be appreciated. She uncovered his eyes and allowed him to take in the sight of the ninety-four-foot waterfall, Ganoga Falls.

"Isn't she beautiful?"

"What makes you think it's a she?"

"Because she's beautiful."

"You don't think men are beautiful?" His eyes crinkled at the corners and he let out a low laugh before pulling her to him. She is beautiful. And you're beautiful. Thank you for bringing me here. I'm glad I get to be here with you. I'm glad to see you out of the house."

"The trail we took is the easiest trail to get here. So, I don't have to hike Falls Trail to get to it. It's peaceful and tranquil. Well, at least on weekdays. There are way too many hikers on the weekends to enjoy it."

"I thought you liked cities and people. Here you are dragging me out on a nature trail. If I didn't know better, I'd think you were the outdoorsy type."

"If you could eliminate the bugs, the dirt, and the rain, then I might consider being an outdoorsy person. I love horses, birds, and waterfalls. Look at this." She spread her arms out and turned in a circle. "How could anyone not love this?"

"They'd have to be crazy. Especially if they could be here with you."

"You're being corny. Stop already."

He laughed again before walking out on a massive boulder and holding his hand out to help her. She joined him on the rock and they sat there on the rock in the creek, allowing the spray from the waterfall hitting the rocks below to shower them with a fine mist. The spray cooled her skin. They'd worked up a sweat on the hike in.

"This is my idea of a real date," she said.

"Now I know what I have to outdo."

"Good luck with that, cowboy." She spun her engagement band on her finger, considering what it would be like to spend the rest of her life with this amazing man.

Chapter 20

*D*awson sat on Claudia's couch, her feet resting in his lap. They'd had an all-day date. He'd taken her to the spa in Scranton. The drive home had left him feeling exhausted, but he'd agreed to watch a movie anyway. He hadn't wanted to leave her.

He stood. "It's about time for me to get going if I'm going hunting in the morning."

"Do you have to go?"

"If I'm going to get a turkey, I do."

"I really enjoyed our date. I'm not ready for it to end."

"I told you, I'd outdo your date."

"I didn't say that yours was better than the one I planned."

"But that's what you meant."

"Ha! I'll give you 'equal', but I'm not saying 'better'," Claudia said.

"I'm glad it was to your liking. I thought it would be. I always knew you were the spa type. Not my thing, but I'm glad you had an enjoyable time."

"We should do it again soon."

"Uh, maybe your sister can go with you next time."

He kissed her and hurried home.

It only took a few minutes to get out his hunting gear: clothes, crossbow, knife, and binoculars. He pulled everything out, making sure nothing was missing.

After a hot shower, he hit the rack. He always looked forward to turkey hunting.

Claudia rolled over again and tried to get comfortable. She hadn't been able to sleep. She watched the clock. *Five o'clock. Maybe she could still get a couple of hours of sleep if she fell asleep now.* The creaky house didn't usually bother her, but every noise sounded like an intruder. She couldn't differentiate squeaky doors and creaky floor boards from the sounds of the house settling or the critters of the night. *That sound was definitely not a mouse.*

In one fluid movement, Claudia retrieved her pistol from under the pillow and sprang out of bed, facing the bedroom door, weapon in hand. She listened carefully for the creaking of the stairs that she'd heard moments before. She crept closer to the door, keeping her weapon trained on the entryway. *Maybe it's Dawson coming out to check on me. Of course, I'm panicked for nothing.*

Standing behind the door with her back to the wall, Claudia inhaled deeply. She let her breath out slowly, as she did that, the bedroom door opened and through the crack in the door, she saw a familiar hulking figure silhouetted in the doorway. She squeezed the trigger only to realize the safety was on. She flipped it off. The man spun toward the sound, his own gun pointed toward the door. A drop of sweat rolled down her forehead despite the chill in the air. She was sure the man could hear her heart beat it was so loud. *This might be my only chance.* Claudia pointed the gun at the hollow interior door and squeezed the trigger. He let out an expletive and shot back. A bullet grazed her shoulder. He yanked at the door and grabbed Claudia's arm, wrenching it behind her body. She struggled to keep hold of her weapon and managed to get off another round. He slammed her hand into the bureau causing her to lose her grip on the pistol. He whacked her hard in the face with his Glock. She tasted blood.

The intruder grabbed a handful of her hair and dragged her out the bedroom door. Pulling her down the hall, he twisted the arm that had been grazed by the bullet. She registered the red stain on her pajama top and wondered how bad the wound was. He threw her down the steps ahead of him. Her head slammed on the posts as she crashed down the steps. The stabbing pain in her head threatened to overtake her, but she forced herself to ignore it and took off running toward the door. Another shot from his gun stopped her progress. His shot shattered the lamp a few feet to her left.

When he reached her, he stuck the gun in her back. "Walk!" He followed her as he forced her to walk through the back gardens and into the cornfield. She stumbled, but kept going. The cold steel of the barrel between her shoulder blades kept her moving. The stalks of corn scratched at her limbs as she struggled to get through it in the dark of the night. She considered diving into the corn, running and hiding among the stalks, but knew he'd take a shot before she could escape. The tiny sliver of moon didn't give them much light, but as they approached the clearing, she could make out a boulder in the woods beyond the edge of the clearing. He pushed her forward and she stumbled before righting herself. Her mind thought back to her training. What should she do in this situation? When they approached the boulder, he shoved her down onto it, then sat beside her. "You're going to pay for that stunt you pulled back there."

Claudia didn't respond. She turned her head, chin lifted. *Lord, help.* The sound of an owl pierced the silence of the night.

Her captor bent down and ripped a piece of his t-shirt off. Claudia watched as he made a tourniquet to stop the bleeding in his lower leg. She hadn't realized he'd been hit. She'd noticed he was limping, but since he was behind her most of the time, she hadn't been able to discern much more than that. How could she exploit his injury for her own benefit? If he hadn't put the tourniquet on, she would've been able to count on blood loss causing him to lose consciousness in time, but he was smarter than that. He would want to move and soon. He probably stopped just long enough to treat his wound.

"Walk down that deer trail." He indicated an overgrown path through the woods where the deer had trampled down the ferns.

He used the muzzle of the gun to push her in the direction of the trail. She complied. A sudden peace fell on her. She believed she'd survive this, but if she didn't she knew she'd be okay.

Thorns kept grabbing at her pajama pants as she tried to navigate the trail. Whenever she would stop to detangle herself, the cold steel of his firearm would encourage her to speed up.

After what felt like hours, but was, in reality, no more than fifteen minutes, he pushed her down onto a fallen log and sat beside her, draping his gun arm around her neck.

"It's almost time. I've been looking forward to this for months. Your body will be found. And I'll leave a trail framing that Dawson boy. He'll be as easy to frame as Johan was. Who would've thought the police would've believed he would dump a body in his own classroom. They must be morons.

"The plan is in motion. Now I need some of your blood to seal the deal. I'll get it worked out, so that he'll not only go down for your murder, but he'll be on the hook for the other unfortunates who had to die. At least Professor Marcus will be cleared.

"Don't you worry your pretty head, dear. You'll soon be with that precious Jesus you talk so much about. I wonder where He is now.

"Makes you think about whether your faith is in vain, doesn't it? Well, you'll soon find out." He grabbed her injured arm and threw her up against a nearby tree with enough force to cause her head to snap back and her vision to go cloudy.

Lord, help me to retain consciousness.

She reached out to the tree to steady herself and the motion increased the blood loss from her arm. "Jesus is with me now. I'm at peace. You can't hurt me."

"Oh, but I can hurt you. Allow me to demonstrate."

He pushed her down to her knees and placed the barrel of the weapon at the base of her skull. "Pray to your God. You're about to meet Him."

The sun had yet to rise, but Dawson, decked out in bright orange and camouflage, crept toward his tree stand as silently as possible. He would be positioned before the turkeys took flight from their roosting place. He didn't intend to head back to the house until he had Thanksgiving dinner secured or dusk descended on him, whichever came first. He slung his bow across his back and worked his way up and into his tree stand. He poured coffee from his thermos into the lid and savored the rich flavor.

Rustling leaves got his attention. He quickly lifted the bow into position and followed the noise. The sun wasn't visible beyond the mountain, but the sky was turning lighter. He spotted a man pushing a woman onto her knees on the narrow deer path to his left. They were about forty yards away, but Dawson saw the gun being raised to the woman's head. His bolt was loaded, and he didn't hesitate. The arrow hit its mark. The man fell. He prayed it hadn't hit the woman. He'd never forgive himself if he'd shot an innocent woman attempting to save her. The man wasn't dead, he lifted his gun again, but the woman kicked it away and took off running. Her movements made it clear. It was his Claudia. He saw the man rise again. He loaded another bolt and kept it trained on him, while he scanned the area to see where Claudia had gone.

She felt the weight of her captor on top of her. She was still alive. She scurried out from under him. He'd been shot in the back, but was alive and repositioning his weapon. She stepped hard on his earlier gunshot wound. He screamed like a goat with hoof rot and relaxed his hand on the weapon. She kicked his gun hand hard. The Glock flew out of his hand. She took off running before he could reclaim his weapon and take chase.

Running as hard as she could, she searched the area for a place to hide. Maybe she could get back to the cornfield. Then she spotted it. She slipped herself into the abandoned coyote den, at least she hoped it was abandoned. She would be safe here. Her heart beat wildly against her ribcage reminding her that she was alive. The hole in the ground wasn't comfortable, but it was a place to hide while she formulated an escape plan. Claudia could see the deer trail from her vantage point, so she kept her eyes trained on it.

She heard a noise at the entrance to the den and turned to greet a coyote face to face. The den wasn't abandoned. The standoff seemed to go on forever. The coyote whined and pawed the ground.

Claudia pleaded with the animal with her eyes. Hoping against hope that it wouldn't attack. It made one more long howling noise and then took off running.

An acrid smoke filled the air. Fire! No wonder the coyote had left. She climbed out of the den and ran toward the deer trail.

Dawson spotted the coyote going back to its den. He'd watched as Claudia hid herself in that hole. It was a tense standoff. He raised his bow, but couldn't get a clear shot of the coyote that would miss Claudia. For several tense moments the two stared at each other, but then the coyote took off in a full sprint. The pungent odor of burning leaves filled his nostrils. He should've taken another shot at the man when he had the chance, he'd taken his eyes off him to watch Claudia, and he'd somehow managed to start a fire. The summer had been a dry one and so far, this autumn, they'd had precious little rain, none in the past several weeks. It wouldn't be long before the smoke was too thick to get through. He pulled his cell phone from his pocket, but there was no signal. How was he going to get help here? He'd have to make a run for the house, but he couldn't leave Claudia out here to fend for herself.

He watched as she pulled herself from the hole and ran toward his house.

He climbed down the ladder to meet her.

Claudia was running as hard as she could, trying to reach the safety of Dawson's house. If she could get there, she could call for help. Someone jumped off the ladder of a tree stand a few feet from her as she ran. Panic gripped her.

Dawson's voice. "Keep running!"

He shouted the words and emphasized them by pushing her in the direction of the house. He stayed behind her, though he could've easily overtaken her and gotten to the house first. She wondered why he didn't do that, so that they could get help faster.

He had a bow slung on his shoulder. Maybe that was hindering his progress. Why didn't he put it down? The smoke was getting thicker and she stumbled over tree roots she hadn't seen. As her lungs filled with smoke she choked and couldn't get enough air to get a decent breath. Dawson placed something over her mouth. Some type of wet fabric. She couldn't think clearly enough to identify what it was. It helped her breathe.

She tried to climb the back steps when she reached the house, but fell on her way up them. Dawson was choking, but he managed to pick her up and get her into the house. He set her down by the back door and collapsed beside her, coughing. He reached for the telephone, but the line was dead. "Now what?" he choked out.

Chapter 21

*D*awson had never been happier to hear the plaintive screech of sirens. He wondered how they'd known. Did someone see the smoke and call? He tried to sit up, but didn't have the energy. Peeking over at Claudia, he noticed her eyes were open, but she appeared to be in shock. She was sucking in short shallow breaths. The look in her eyes terrified him. He'd never expected to have to see her fight for her life the way she had out there.

The paramedics came into the kitchen and checked them both out insisting that they go to the hospital. He tried to tell them that there was a serial killer outside, who had set fire to the woods, but his words were a jumble of confusion. The men nodded as if they understood and moved them along toward the ambulance.

When they were finally in the hospital and were thinking more clearly, he asked for an officer to come talk to him. He explained the situation in more detail. The officer agreed to follow-up. He figured the suspect wouldn't have gotten far having been shot in the back with a crossbow. They would set up a perimeter and hopefully catch the guy by sundown. Dawson hoped they did, but he wouldn't trust Claudia's safety to them. He'd find another way to keep his fiancé out of harm's way, if they failed.

Sirens everywhere. It wasn't safe to get away yet. He'd have to find a way out of here and get better treatment for his injuries, but how could he do that without arousing suspicion. He had to make it sound like a hunting accident. The only way to do that was to go somewhere where he belonged. His own place, but if he did that, the police might want to check out his place. They'd get a warrant for the grounds. He didn't want that. They'd find his book. And his trophies. Unless he got there first and destroyed them. Or hid them. He couldn't destroy year's worth of work. Memories.

What were his other options? As he leaned against the enormous oak tree and watched the fire blaze, he wondered if his plans were for naught. Would the fire burn out of control and catch up with him before he could plan his getaway? Memories of his childhood flooded back. His grandmother serving milk and cookies on Sunday after church. There were warm memories. But they rarely came to mind anymore. Now he thought of the pain of losing his family. The charred bodies of his wife and children. Now he might die in a fire just as they had. How fitting.

How had he let Claudia get away? He'd had everything planned out in detail. He'd done everything perfectly for so long, but today he had messed up. His calculations had been for naught. He'd underestimated his target. He should've let this one go. He'd been due to switch towns months ago. He shouldn't have stuck around Pennsylvania. He'd seen the crime shows. They said the killer always makes a mistake. This was his.

Holding his balled-up shirt tightly against his wound and leaning against the tree to put pressure on the other side, he cursed. A noise got his attention. Raising his head, he saw a man pointing a pistol on him. The man was dressed in camouflage and grinning like a clown. He looked incredibly happy. "I got you now. You mess with one Marine, you mess with us all."

"Oh, God." The irony of calling out to a god he claimed not to believe in was not lost on him.

He watched as the man squeezed the trigger.

Dawson glanced up as Jason entered his room.

"Hey. How are you?"

"Ready to get out of here."

"I'll bet. I'm sure they'll release you soon. I thought you might want an update on the case."

Dawson hit the button on the bed to sit up straighter. "Please. I can't get any information from these guys." He indicated the cops standing outside his door.

"Well, as I'm sure you know, state police were first law enforcement on the scene, since you don't have locals out your way. Fire fighters, were already there and game commission officers showed up shortly after. We worked together to comb the fields of the McIntyre and Montgomery farms collecting what little evidence made it through the fire.

"The game commission has a case against whoever set the woods on fire, threatening local wildlife. The fire fighters wanted to make sure the fire was out and wouldn't start back up from embers left burning. And we, needed to gather evidence against the suspect we'd taken into custody.

"When the men came to a grove of oak trees, they found a man leaning against it. He'd been shot through with an arrow, shot in the leg, and shot in the head. It appears the head shot was the fatal one. The coroner will make that determination for sure. He would've died from the bolt, but the second shooter killed him first."

"Wow, that's a significant update. Who is this suspect you'd taken into custody?"

"That part is strange."

"Lay it on me."

"When they stormed the cabin, they found an unconscious man in military fatigues. He didn't appear to have any injuries, so he definitely lost consciousness from smoke inhalation. When he came to, he told us he was on a mission."

"A mission?"

"Claimed he was sent to watch Claudia. To keep her safe."

"Who sent him?"

"It doesn't look like anyone actually sent him. We looked him up. He's an Iraqi war vet with severe PTSD. He's been in and out of the VA hospital. He did work with Claudia's unit a year ago. We think he must've met her there and somehow attached himself to her. He seems to believe that he had a mission and that now that he killed the man bothering her, he's completed his mission."

"Wow. So that's the squatter I wasn't able to catch on the game cameras?"

"He was well trained. Sniper. If he'd wanted to do either of you harm, you'd be dead."

"I'm glad he decided to be on our side."

"That's the spirit. We'll see if we can get him readmitted to the VA Hospital."

"That sounds like a wise choice."

"We're going to have to take statements from you and Claudia, but I can put Mac off until morning."

"Thanks. I doubt she'll be up to it now."

Claudia smiled broadly when Jason entered the room. "Dawson told me everything."

"I have the latest information." He sat down at her bedside. "I'm officially here to take both of your statements, but as your brother-in-law, I'm here to keep you in the loop."

"Spill it."

"Dawson was in the hall talking to a nurse, he'll be in shortly. Let's wait until he joins us, so I don't have to repeat myself."

"You're killing me!"

Dawson walked in and joined her bedside, leaning down to kiss her as he did. "I'm sprung, but they have to wait for your breathing test before they'll spring you."

"Ugh. Now you're both killing me. Let's hear it, Jas."

"Hear what?" Dawson asked.

"I have news on the killer. We made a match to the DNA found on your tire to him. But that's not the interesting part. That same DNA was found in unsolved murders in several other states. This man has been at this for some time."

"Are you serious? I wouldn't have suspected Professor Borneo. Thought he was a good teacher. A normal guy. Until yesterday."

"That name would've been helpful to have sooner, but we were able to get it from the identification in his pocket. They checked his cabin and found a kill book. It's scary stuff. Dawson's theory was correct. He was targeting Christians. Some sort of vendetta against God for killing his family."

"Wow. That's insane. I wonder how soon Sofie's professor friend will get cleared."

"I couldn't say, but it shouldn't be too long. So, now, I do have to take your statements. We need to have them on file. Okay?"

"By now, I could give a statement in my sleep. I probably have."

Epilogue

The wedding was spectacular. She wore a satin gown with a train that trailed behind her. It was her something old. It had been her mother's. Decorating her neckline was another something old. A glittering emerald on a gold chain. A gift from Dawson. It had been his great grandmother's jewel.

The two had more than one good-natured argument over the wedding. She wanted a big beautiful wedding with everyone she knew in attendance. He didn't care about the size of the wedding, but wanted to marry quickly. She didn't think they would have time to plan her perfect wedding and still get married that soon.

They compromised. He enlisted help from one of his clients, a wealthy businessman who owned an island in the Caribbean. The man provided all they could ever want, and Dawson only needed to fly out their friends and family. Claudia thought the expense was too much, but Dawson assured her that they could afford it.

Now here she stood at the back of the chapel preparing to walk down the aisle and become Mrs. Dawson Montgomery. Tears filled her eyes as she proceeded down the aisle, her father's hand on her arm. He put her hand in Dawson's before taking his spot in front of them. This was a dream moment. If only her mother were around to witness it. "Do you, Dawson Montgomery, take this woman, Claudia McIntyre, to be your lawfully wedded wife, in sickness and in health, 'til death do you part?"

"I do." She heard Dawson speak the words and her breath stopped for a moment.

"Do you, Claudia McIntyre, take this man, Dawson Montgomery, to be your lawfully wedded husband, in sickness and in health, 'til death do you part?"

"I do." There was no hesitation. She was ready to spend the rest of her life with the man she loved.

Coming Soon

*The third and final book in the
Endless Mountain Series*

Chasing Sofie

ofie slammed the car door and marched to Johan's office. Taking a deep breath, she calmed herself before knocking. Sitting in a hot car for twenty minutes waiting for him was unacceptable. How infuriatingly inconsiderate. No answer came as she waited at the door, seething. He must've forgotten they had a date. What else was new? Pushing open the door, she froze in place. When her senses returned she let out a high pitch scream. She heard the sounds of running feet, but remained glued to the floor. Johan was in no shape for their date.

"Someone get her out of here. Janet, call the police." She heard a male voice say. She heard someone running down the hall and assumed it was Janet, not wanting to walk past Johan's body to make the call from the desk.

"Sofie, right?" A robust woman Sofie recognized as a biology professor put her arm around her and physically turned her body, so she was facing back out into the corridor. "You're in shock. Let's get you a glass of water and you can splash some cold water on your face."

Sofie barely nodded her head. Words eluded her.

"I'm Marsha. I'll wait with you until the police come. I'm sure they are going to want to speak with you."

She let herself be led to another room down the hall. Where she was taken to a sink. Her hands would not obey her commands as she tried to turn the faucet on. Trembling, she started to slide to the floor, but Marsha lifted her back up and held her against her ample bosom. "Oh sweetheart, you shouldn't have had to see that. I'm so sorry you witnessed that scene. Were you here for a meeting with the professor?" How could she find the words to tell this kind woman that Johan wasn't her professor, but her boyfriend? They'd been living together for two years. No words came out. It didn't matter. Her words would return eventually. How could this have happened?

She heard voices from down the hall. They weren't trying to be quiet.

"Obviously, it was a suicide. There's no doubt about it," she heard the man from earlier say.

"We can leave that for the police detectives to decide. I'm sure you'd agree?" another man said.

"Of, course. But I think it looks rather clear. It's unfortunate that the young lady had to find him like that."

"I know. What a shame."

She wanted to scream that she wasn't that young. How could she make them see her pain wasn't simply shock at finding a professor dead? Still, no words would come. She pulled her cell from her purse and with trembling hands, unlocked the screen. She showed the screen to Marsha. The background picture was her and Johan snuggled up in a corner booth at their favorite pizza joint. The moment the realization struck the other woman, Sofie could tell. There was a sharp intake of breath, followed by the woman stroking her hair. Marsha wet a paper towel and held it to her forehead. It was cool and felt good. It wasn't long after when a police oiificer entered the biology lab and spoke with Marsha, who explained the situation to him. She turned back to Sofie and told her to go with the man. Sofie hoped her words would return to her by the time she was to give her statement. She followed the man to an office and he pulled out two chairs and motioned for her to sit. He reached into his pocket and took out a small notebook. After asking her permission to record the conversation, he took out his telephone and opened a recording app. As he set his phone on the desk, his eyes met hers.

"I understand that your name is Sofie. Is that correct?"

Telling herself she had to make words come out she squeaked out a "yes."

"I'm sorry, but can you speak up?" he asked.

Marsha appeared in the doorway. "She's in shock. You may have to give her a few minutes to compose herself."

The man rose and spoke to Marsha for a moment before closing the office door.

"Let's try again. I don't want to pressure you. Really, I don't. I do have to find out what you saw when you opened that door. We can be quick about it and I'll send you on your way. You'll need to come to the station and sign a statement, but the more you tell me now, the better."

She took out her own notebook with trembling hands and wrote down the words. "He was hanging from the curtains. My boyfriend was dead."

He raised his eyebrows slightly. "Okay. That's good. You can write what you know. That will be very helpful. You can call with more information if it comes to you. Simply write down your statement. Everything you did and saw, include why you were here, what you were doing, and how you came upon the body. Then, I'll get someone to take you home."

She wrote. "I have my car."

"Sweetie, you're in no condition to drive."

It was then that she realized that her home was no longer her home. She'd been living with him. That wouldn't be an option now. She was sure she could return to get her stuff, but his family would want her out. Where would she go?

Dear Reader,

I hope you enjoyed reading book two of the Endless Mountain Series, *Implicating Claudia.* Please check out some of my other titles, including the next book in the series, *Chasing Sofie,* which will be available soon.

If you enjoyed *Implicating Claudia,* the most helpful thing you can do is leave an honest review. So, please consider submitting a review on Amazon and/or GoodReads. It doesn't cost anything other than a moment of your time and can be tremendously beneficial to me. Your quick review helps to get my book into the hands of other readers who may enjoy it.

https://www.amazon.com/gp/product/B076CGN4B9/
https://www.goodreads.com/book/show/41718938-implicating-claudia

For a list of my current books and upcoming releases check out the novel page on my website: https://www.elleekay.com/novels/

Thank you.
Elle E. Kay
https://www.elleekay.com

About Elle E. Kay

Elle E. Kay lives in the Back Mountain area of Pennsylvania. She loves life in the country on her little farmette. Elle is a born-again Christian with a deep faith and love for the Lord Jesus Christ. She desires to live for Him and to put Him first in everything she does.

She writes children's books under the name Ellie Mae Kay.

Be sure to sign up for Elle's newsletter at https://elleekay.com/newsletter-sign-up/. You can also connect with Elle on her website and blog at https://www.elleekay.com/.

Or you can follow her on social media at:
    Bookbub: https://www.bookbub.com/profile/elle-e-kay
    Facebook: https://www.facebook.com/ElleEKay7
    Twitter: https://twitter.com/ElleEKay7
    Pinterest: https://www.pinterest.com/elleekay7/
    Google+: https://plus.google.com/u/0/+ElleEKay
    Amazon Author Central: http://www.amazon.com/author/ellekay
    Instagram: https://www.instagram.com/elleekay7/
    Goodreads:
    https://www.goodreads.com/author/show/15016833.Elle_E_Kay

Acknowledgements

I would like to give special thanks to my editor, Patti Geesey, who offered her expertise and critical eye to make my work shine brighter. Any errors or deficiencies are my own.

Thank you to my husband, Joe, for putting up with the long hours of writing and editing.

This story is a product of my imagination and a work of fiction. Names, characters, businesses, places, events, locales, and incidents are either the products of my imagination or in the case of actual towns, historical persons, and companies mentioned, they have been used in a fictitious manner. Any resemblance to actual persons, living or dead, or actual events is purely coincidental.

Any errors or deficiencies are my own.

Personal Testimony

I first came to know Jesus as a young teen, but before long I strayed from God and allowed my selfish desires to rule me. I sought after acceptance and love from my peers, not knowing that only God could fill my emptiness. My teen years were full of angst and misery, for me and my family. People I loved were hurt by my selfishness. My heartache was at times overwhelming, but I couldn't find the healing I desperately desired. After several runaway attempts my family was left with little choice, and they put me in a group home/residential facility where I would get the constant supervision I needed.

At that home I met a godly man called 'Big John' who tried once again to draw me back to Jesus. He would point out Matthew 11:28-30 and remind me that all I had to do to find peace was give my cares to Christ. I wanted to live a Christian life, but something kept pulling me away. The cycle continued well into adulthood. I would call out to God, but then I would turn away from Him. (If you read the old-testament you'll see that the nation of Israel had a similar pattern, they would call out to God and He would heal them and bring them back into their land. Then they would stray and He would chastise them. It was a cycle that went on and on).

When I came to realize that God's love was still available to me despite all my failings, I found peace and joy that have remained with me to do this day. It wasn't God who kept walking away. He'd placed his seal on me in childhood and no matter how far I ran from Him, **He remained faithful.** When I finally recognized His unfailing love, I was made free.

2 Timothy 2:13

"If we believe not, yet he abideth faithful: he cannot deny himself."

Ephesians 4:30

"And grieve not the holy Spirit of God, whereby ye are sealed unto the day of redemption."

I let myself be drawn into His loving arms and led by His precious nail-scarred hands. He has kept me securely at His side and taught me important life lessons. Jesus has given me back the freedom I had in Christ on that day when I accepted the precious gift He'd offered. My life in Him is so much fuller than it ever was when I tried to live by the world's standards.

I implore you, if you've known Jesus and strayed, call out to Him.

If you've never know Jesus Christ as your personal Lord and Saviour. Find out what it means to have a relationship with Christ. Not religion, but a personal relationship with a loving God.

God makes it clear in His word that there isn't a person righteous enough to get to heaven on their own.

Romans 3:10

"As it is written, There is none righteous, no, not one:"

We are all sinners.

Romans 3:23

For all have sinned, and come short of the glory of God;

Death is the penalty for sin.

Romans 6:23

"For the wages of sin is death; but the gift of God is eternal life through Jesus Christ our Lord."

Christ died on the cross for our sins.

Romans 5:8

"But God commendeth his love toward us, in that, while we were yet sinners, Christ died for us."

If we confess and believe we will be saved.

Romans 10:9

"That if thou shalt confess with thy mouth the Lord Jesus, and shalt believe in thine heart that God hath raised him from the dead, thou shalt be saved."

Once we believe he sets us free.

Romans 8:1

"There is therefore now no condemnation to them which are in Christ Jesus, who walk not after the flesh, but after the Spirit."

I hope you'll take hold of that freedom and start a personal relationship with Christ Jesus.

www.ingramcontent.com/pod-product-compliance
Lightning Source LLC
Chambersburg PA
CBHW021022120726
47905CB00009B/3131